Augustin Daly, Gustav von Moser

The Passing Regiment

A comedy of the day, in five acts

Augustin Daly, Gustav von Moser

The Passing Regiment
A comedy of the day, in five acts

ISBN/EAN: 9783337103590

Printed in Europe, USA, Canada, Australia, Japan

Cover: Foto ©Andreas Hilbeck / pixelio.de

More available books at **www.hansebooks.com**

PASSING REGIM

A COMEDY OF THE DAY, IN FIVE A

(From the G   d Frans

AS ACTE

PRINTE

DRAMATIS PERSONÆ AND ORIGINAL CAST.

MR. LINTHICUM WINTHROP, the amiable representative of
   one of the F. F.'s of Narragansett Pier . . MR. W. J. LE MOYNE
MRS. MELINDA WINTHROP, his wife; a whole flood of New
   England Sunshine in herself . . . . . . MRS. G. H. GILBERT
TELKA ESSOFF, their niece; a Russian Heiress; a bit of Mus-
   covite Ice and Impulse . . . . MISS ADA REHAN
MR. PEREGRINE BUNKER, Chairman of the Regimental Re-
   ception Committee; and entire Committee in his own
   person . . . . MR. CHARLES LECLERCQ
MRS. MATHILDA BUNKER, his help-meet in more senses
   than one . . . . MISS MAY SILVIE
LINDA, their daughter; with a disbelief in Love at First Sight
   and an experience to the contrary . . . MISS MARIE WILLIAMS
ROTH HOFFMEISTER, the new Apothecary of the thriving
   Township of Narragansett Pier . . . . MR. JAMES LEWIS
COLONEL VAN KLEEK, of the Excelsior Regiment, N. G. S.
   N. Y. . . . . MR. GEORGE PARKES
DOLF VAN TASSELL, M.D., Regimental Surgeon of the same,
                                             MR. DIGBY BELL
MILLY MERRITT, the demure young companion of the Rus-
   sian Heiress, and in possession of a secret concerning the
   aforesaid Surgeon, which, with the characteristic open-
   heartedness of her sex, she proceeds to divulge in the
   opening lines of the play . . . . MISS MAY FIELDING
PAUL DEXTER, Adjutant, etc., of the Excelsior Regiment,
   N. G. S. N. Y. . . . . MR. JOHN DREW
THORPE SYDAM, Lieutenant, etc. . . . . . . MR. HARRY M. PITT
MARY ANNE, cook at Winthrop's . . . . . MISS BLANCHE WEAVER
SOPHIE, maid at the same . . . . MISS EMILY DENIN
JANE, ditto at Bunker's . . . . MISS HAPGOOD
SOLOMON, Winthrop's Butler . . . . MR. E. P. WILKS
SCIPIO, the Adjutant's Man . . . . MR. W. H. BEEKMAN
THE BUGLER, an important functionary at an important crisis,
                                             MR. MILTON

FIRST ACT.

PARLORS AT WINTHROP'S.—The Regiment is invited. "Is Love at First Sight a Dream or a Reality?"

———

SECOND ACT.

THE SAME SCENE.—The Regiment comes to Town. "It is a Reality."

———

THIRD ACT.

AT MR. PEREGRINE BUNKER'S.—The Regiment makes itself at home. "No! it is a Dream."

———

FOURTH ACT.

GROUNDS AND SUMMER HOUSE AT WINTHROP'S.—The Regiment makes Love and is Lost! "Love at Second Sight is Better!"

———

FIFTH ACT.

PARLORS AT WINTHROP'S.—The Regiment prepares to depart. "Several proposals and a Single Rejection."

ACT I.

SCENE.—*Stage represents a front and back parlor in a country house. Mirror, C., in back, window, R., piano. Before curtain rises piano is heard playing, to which music curtain rises.*

MILLY *discovered, R., playing, absorbed.* SOLOMON *enters, C. L., cautiously, with letters and papers, and coughs to attract her attention.*

Solomon. Ahem!

Milly. [*Without turning.*] What is it, Solomon?

Sol. [*Whispers.*] Letters, miss.

Mil. [*Jumps up.*] Is there one for me?

Sol. Yes, miss. [*Gives letter.*]

Mil. [*Aside. Joyfully.*] It's from Dolf! [*Aloud.*] Have you anything else?

Sol. There's one for Miss Telka. [*Looks at it.*] With the foreign stamps as usual. I suppose, now, that comes millions of miles?

Mil. [*Takes the letter.*] Not quite! It's from Russia. Have you seen Miss Telka this morning?

Sol. I saw her half an hour ago.

Mil. Where is she?

Sol. In the mill pond by this time, I guess.

Mil. What?

Sol. I was going to the post-office when I see her tearing down the hill behind her ponies like mad. I didn't have the heart to look where she went.

Mil. [*Relieved.*] There's no fear. She knows how to handle them.

Sol. So she does, miss. She's always in the stable, and every beast in it knows her. But for all that, take my advice, and don't let her drive you. There'll be an accident some day. [*Going up.*] A pitcher that goes too often to the well is sure to be run away with. [*Exits, C. L.*]

Mil. [R., *looks at her letter.*] Shall I keep it until I lock myself in my own room? No! I must read a little—just the commencement—to see what— [*Opens, reads.*] "Darling Milly." [*Kisses and looks at it.*] Why, it's very short. [*Looks round and reads.*] "Our regiment is to pass through Narragansett Pier to-morrow on our way to camp at Newport, and we have had a pressing invitation from the town-people to stop over for a day or two. It is not yet decided if we shall. But if we don't, I'll apply for leave of absence and fly to your arms. A thousand kisses from your devoted husband." [*Startles herself by pronouncing last word, looks round.*] Oh! good gracious, I hope no one heard me. If they should discover that we are married! [*Stage*, R.]

TELKA *enters, excited, carrying wisp of hay*, C. L.

Telka. Where *is* uncle? [*Throws her hat one side.*]
Mil. [R.] Why, Telka! What have you got in your hand?
Tel. [*Offers it.*] Hay. Oblige me by tasting it.
Mil. [*Recoils.*] Hay!
Tel. [L. C.] Well, then, just smell it. It's mouldy. [*Puts it to Mil.'s nose and then to her own.*] Pah! And my ponies are expected to eat stuff like that. I just want to show it to uncle. [*Lays it on table*, L.] And just see the oats. [*Dives in her pocket and produces handful.*] There! [*Blows at them.*] Half of it chaff! And the rest split! Just look for yourself. [*Extends hand for inspection.*]
Mil. [*Not much affected*, R.] I suppose it's very bad, but I really can't tell good oats.
Tel. I can. And such feed is an outrage. [*Crosses to* R., *throws oats on carpet, sees Mil.'s letter.*] What's that?
Mil. [*Folding and hiding it.*] Oh, nothing, only a matter of business.
Tel. What kind of business makes you blush up so. You are hiding that letter.
Mil. Don't be too inquisitive.
Tel. [*Hurt.*] I'm not inquisitive. I'm disappointed. Didn't we swear to be brothers? And the very first thing you have a secret from me. [*Goes up.*]
Mil. My dear—
Tel. [*Down*, L.] Never mind.
Mil. Telka!
Tel. [*Goes up.*] Let me alone.
Mil. [*Produces Tel.'s letter.*] Well, then, here's a letter for you.
Tel. [*Delighted, comes down.*] For me?
Mil. From your father.
Tel. [*Kisses and opens it.*] From my darling papa, and written in my dear old Russian! [*Reads.*] "Moya lubiazna galubka."
Mil. What does that mean?

Tel. Oh, you don't know Russian. That means "my sweetest dove." Papa always calls me that. He loves me so much.

PEREGRINE BUNKER *appears,* C. L., *he enters hurriedly, stops.*

Bunker. [*A bustling, busy man.*] Oh, I beg pardon. That is, good morning, ladies.
Mil. [R.] Pray come in, Mr. Bunker.
Bun. [C.] Thanks, thanks, I've no time, very sorry.
Tel. [L.] Didn't you bring Linda with you?
Bun. Yes, I hope she won't be in the way.
Tel. What an idea!
Bun. Well, then, I'll leave her while I run to the pier. [*Looks at watch.*] Call for her in half an hour. Most obedient, ladies. [*Disappears,* C. L.]
Tel. He talks of his daughter as if she were five years old.
Mil. I believe he thinks she is. [*Goes up and gets to table,* L.]

BUNKER *re-appears.*

Bunker. Here she is. [*To Linda, outside.*] Run right in, my dear. [*To ladies.*] Good morning. [*Exits,* C. L.]

LINDA *enters,* C. L., *merrily, kisses Tel., gives hand to Mil.*

Linda. Papa's on the rush as usual. Not a minute to spare.
Mil. [*At table,* L.] We are used to it.
Linda. [R.] But I got him to stop here with me notwithstanding.
Mil. [*Aside, at table.*] I must send a line to Dolf at once. [*Sits to write.*]
Linda. [*Gives book to Tel.*] Here's your book, Telka. Ever so much obliged.
Tel. [*Takes it and sits.*] Oh, "Lorna Doone." [*Crosses to* R.] How did you like it? Isn't Blackmore delightful. [*Puts book on piano.*]
Linda. [*Puts her hat on table,* L.] Oh, yes. But let me tell you, he don't know the first thing about love.
Tel. [R.] Why not?
Linda. Why, just think! His hero and heroine see one another for the first time and fall in love—over head and ears! madly! on the spot!
Tel. [*Calmly.*] Well, what of that?
Linda. What nonsense! It's so unnatural. One must know a person well before one can love with such devotion. Love don't seize a person all of a sudden like a fever. [*Crosses to* R.]

Tel. [*Animatedly.*] Yes it does! Just exactly like a fever; accompanied with delirium and palpitation of the heart. I can tell you all about it.

Linda. You! Are you in love?

Tel. [*Crosses to* R., *with majesty.*] I was once! For twenty-four consecutive hours.

Linda. [*Confidentially.*] Oh! tell me all about it.

Tel. [*Gravely.*] You promise never to breathe a syllable?

Linda. [*Solemnly.*] On my word and honor.

Tel. [*As they draw nearer, confidentially.*] Well, then, when I was at school, at Madam Storr's, I had a most intimate friend. She graduated a year before me. She was to go home, and we were almost broken-hearted at parting. Her brother came for her. I met him. It was such a moment as never comes but once in a lifetime. An electric shock passed through me, and when I looked in his eyes, I saw just as plain as could be that it had passed through him too.

Linda. Is it possible? Have you seen him since?

Tel. Not by daylight. ˙

Linda. What do you mean?

Tel. I dream of him. His name is Paul, and I know that he loves me. [*Crosses to* L.]

Linda. [*Pettishly.*] I don't believe in it at all. A perfect stranger whom you meet for the first time—

Tel. [*Quickly.*] That's it, the instant you see one another you don't seem to be strangers. You feel as if you had been acquainted forever.

Linda. It's all imagination.

Tel. My dear, you know nothing about it.

Linda. [*Crosses to* C.] I'll leave it to Milly.

Mil. [*Writing.*] What is it? Boarding-school—electric shock? Excuse me, I have an important letter to write.

WINTHROP *enters,* R. U. E.

Tel. [*Rising.*] Here's uncle. We'll ask him. [*Runs up and brings him down.*]

Linda. [*Goes to* Win. *and shakes hands.*] You know, don't you, uncle.

Winthrop. Know what, my dears?

Linda. [L.] Suppose you were to meet a man for the first time.

Win. Very good.

Tel. [*Gets on other side of him,* R.] No, no. Suppose—suppose you were to meet a woman for the first time—a very handsome woman.

Win. I prefer that.

Linda. A woman whom you knew nothing about.

Win. Yes.

Linda. Now, what would happen?

Win. [*Puzzled.*] What would—? [*Pauses.*]

Linda. Would you immediately have an attack of fever?

Win. Fever?

Tel. She don't mean that.

Linda. Well, an electric shock?

Win. I'm afraid I don't quite understand you.

Tel. [*Irritated, turns him round to face her.*] The question is this, uncle, do you believe in love at first sight?

Win. [*Sharply.*] What, what?

Linda. [*Turning him to face her.*] Or is it essential that one should know the person some time previously?

Tel. [*Exalted, turning to him.*] Does love strike like the lightning?

Linda. [*Turning him.*] Or is it the growth of a mutual esteem?

Both. Give us your opinion.

Win. [*Smiles.*] It is truly refreshing to see this thirst for knowledge.

Tel. [*Impatiently.*] Answer, uncle, answer.

Win. Presently. Answer me a question first. [*To Tel.*] How old are you?

Tel. Why, you know—eighteen.

Win. [*To Linda.*] And you?

Linda. Seventeen.

Win. Very well. Go on playing with you dolls and doll houses and come to me in a year. [*Crosses to* R.]

Tel. It's impossible to talk sense with you, uncle. Come, Linda. We are very angry. [*Going, and taking Linda's arm,* L.]

Linda. Yes, indeed we are.

Tel. [*To Linda.*] I'll tell you what we'll do, we'll send the question to the "Ladies Bazaar." [*Exeunt,* R. U. E., *skipping.*]

Win. [*Severely, advancing,* C.] Miss Merritt!

Mil. [*Rising.*] Yes, sir.

Win. [R.] Can you inform me how these girls came to ask such questions?

Mil. [*Coming down,* L.] Why, Mr. Winthrop, young girls always take an interest in such matters.

Win. They've been reading more novels.

Mil. I believe they have.

Win. It won't do for Telka to fill her head with such stuff. You must see to it. I selected you for her companion because I considered your sedate conversation would be a corrective of her tendency to wildness.

Mil.   You are too good.

Win.   [*Relaxing.*] You are really very sedate for one so young and pretty.

MRS. WINTHROP *enters*, R. D.

Mrs. Winthrop.   [*To Win.*] My dear!

Win.   [*Changing tone.*] Hem! So, Miss Merritt, you will please attend to the matter. [MIL. *goes up.*]

Mrs. W.   What is it, my dear.

Win.   I was speaking about Telka.

Mrs. W.   Oh. [*Crosses to table, and•sees hay on it.*] Good gracious, who left this stuff on the table? Hay.

Win.   [*Concurring, following her.*] So it is—hay.

Mrs. W.   [*Looks down.*] And oats all over the carpet. [*Gathers her skirts about her.*]

Win.   Oats, undoubtedly.

Mil.   [*Down* R.] Telka brought them in.

Mrs. W.   [*To Mil., coldly.*] Please have them removed. The room looks like a stable. [*Crosses, gives hay to Mil.*]

Win.   Exactly like a stable.

Mil.   I'll send the servant. [*Exits*, R. D.]

Mrs. W.   Your niece turns the house topsy-turvy with her pranks. I don't know what possessed us to take such a burden on our backs.

Win.   My dear, it couldn't be avoided. Telka is your poor sister's only child, and to make some amends for marrying a Russian, she desired her daughter to be brought up an American. Her father very kindly sent her to us from his icy wilderness, when we begged him as a favor to do so.

Mrs. W.   [*Softened, but still vexed.*] Of course! I like the girl, in fact, I'm quite fond of her.

Win.   [L., *authoritatively.*] Nevertheless we must check her. She is getting too full of notions. A little while ago she wanted to know what I thought about love. It's these infernal Seaside novels.

Mrs. W.   Why shouldn't a young creature read good novels? I'm sure woman's life is weary enough.

Win.   [*Concurring.*] Quite so, quite so.

Mrs. W.   [*Melancholy, sighs.*] When *I* was a girl, the future appeared to me [*Crosses to* L.] far different from what I find it day by day.

Win.   Exactly. Let's change the subject.

Mrs. W. [L.] You always change the subject when I talk of my youth.

Win. My dear, we've both changed *that* subject a long time ago.

BUNKER *enters*, C. L., *quickly.*

Bunker. Ah! There you are! So glad to find you both at home. Most important intelligence. [*Puts hat on table.*] By the way, my daughter's not gone? [*Looks round.*]

Mrs. W. She's in the garden with Telka.

Bun. [*Wipes forehead, to Mrs. W.*] I'm going to give *you* a surprise.

Win. [R.] What has happened?

Bun. [*To Mr. W.*] You'll be astonished.

Win. I'm astonished already. Out with it.

Bun. I knew they'd accept our invitation.

Mrs. W. You make me quite anxious. Pray tell us.

Bun. Of course I'll tell you, but just let me catch my breath. I'm overworked. [*Looks at his hand.*] What did I change that ring on my finger for? [*Meditates over it.*] Oh, yes. [*Suddenly.*] The hotel for the band. I must attend to it at once. [*Seizes hat and about to go.*]

Mrs. W. At least, before you go, tell us what you came for?

Bun. [C., *returns, smiling.*] Sure enough. Well, you *will* be surprised.

Mrs. W. Oh! for the patience of Job.

Bun. Prepare yourself. You remember reading a report that the celebrated Excelsior Regiment from New York, which is going to camp at Newport, was to pass through our place. Well, a committee of our citizens, after a deal of correspondence and persuasion, have induced them to stop over at Narragansett Pier and afford us the pleasure of entertaining them.

Mrs. W. Entertaining them? Where, pray?

Bun. Where? Why in our houses—we've organized a reception committee and distributed the gallant fellows all over the place. [*Looks at watch.*]

Mrs. W. Why, they are expected in Newport on Friday.

Bun. [C.] Yes—and they'll be here to-day. So you can imagine the work. I'm chairman of the reception committee. Everything is to be arranged in the next few hours. [*Looks at watch.*] I can't stop another moment. Good day! [*Going—returns.*] Oh—please send my Linda home before lunch, will you? Thanks! Good day! [*Exits*, C. L.]

Mrs. W. [*Crosses to Win.*] You never told me a word about this.

Win. I didn't think the regiment had accepted our invitation.

BUNKER *re-enters*, C. L.

Bunker. [c.] I forgot the most important thing. Here's your list. [*Gives slip of paper.* MRS. W. *gets back to* L.]

Win. [*Takes paper and puts on glasses to read it.*] ·My list?

Bun. Yes. List of the officers you are expected to receive and entertain.

Mrs. W. You are not going to quarter soldiers on us.

Bun. [*Reads billet in* Win.'s *hands.*] Why not? Of course I am. Winthrop's on the committee. He's got to take his share of 'em; you've got four officers—lieutenants.

Mrs. W. [*Holds up her hands.*] Mercy!

Win. Four officers!

Bun. By rights you ought to take more. Your house is so large; and you ought to have had a company of privates, your grounds are so roomy! But I saved you the annoyance, and got you only four. Nothing like having a friend as chairman of the committee. [*Takes his hand.*]

Win. [*Shakes hands feebly.*] I hope I may be able to do as much for you some day.

Bun. [*Warmly.*] Don't mention it. [*Converses with Mrs. W.*]

TELKA *and* LINDA *run in*, R. U. E.

Linda. [*To Bun.*] Oh, papa, is it true the soldiers are going to stop with us? [*They converse.*]

Tel. Oh, uncle! Won't it be lovely! I do hope you'll get some, too.

Win. [*Nettled.*] Perhaps you'd like the whole regiment!

Tel. Oh, it will be just splendid. I'll show off my ponies, and take the officers out driving. You insist on nice-looking ones, too, uncle; don't let them put you off with any kind. Pick them out for yourself.

Win. There, don't bother me. [*Goes to table,* L.]

Tel. [*To Mrs. W.*] Aunt, *you* see that we have lots of soldiers. If there isn't room, I'll sleep with Milly.

Mrs. W. Don't worry me, child.

Tel. I think you are both very cross with me.

Linda. [*As she and* BUN. *go to rear.*] Come here, Telka, papa knows all about it.

Tel. [*To Bun., going with them.*] Are there any cannon coming?

Bun. [*Going.*] Nonsense—no. No cannon.

Linda. But the bands are coming?

Bun. Certainly.

Tel. [*Ecstatically.*] *Oh!* Won't it be delightful! I hope they'll stay ever so long! Months! [*Exeunt,* C. L.]

Win. [*To Mrs. W.*] We are in for it. How do you like the prospect?

Mrs. W. I don't know why you should go on so about it. It's a trouble, of course, but it's a change.

Win. I'm perfectly contented as I am.

Mrs. W. What worries me is—we've only got two spare rooms.

Win. The spare rooms don't worry me. What about Telka?

Mrs. W. Well—what about Telka?

Win. She can't stay here with a whole staff of officers quartered in the house.

Mrs. W. We can't send her away.

Win. No—it's too late.

Mrs. W. What are you afraid of?

Win. You know what these young drawing-room soldiers are. They'll all pay her attention. She may fall in love—and we'll have the responsibility.

Mrs. W. How you talk. The girl is no longer a child.

Win. [*Struck.*] I have an idea. [*Rises.*] We can pretend she *is,* and put her in short frocks.

Mrs. W. [*Rises.*] You are ridiculous.

Win. Well, then, do me one favor. Don't let them know that she's so enormously rich. Pass her off as a poor relation. It may be the saving of her.

Mrs. W. [*Rising.*] There's some wisdom in that. But now let's arrange about the house and see what is to be done. That's the first thing.

Win. Yes—let's prepare to swallow our pill. [*Going,* R.]

Mrs. W. [*To* SOL., *who enters,* C. L.] Send up Mary Anne and Sophie. [SOL. *exits,* C. L. *To* WIN.] And now, my dear, I shall want some money,

Win. Money? Money?

Mrs. W. [*Sharply.*] You don't think my allowance will cover all these extras, do you?

Win. [*Going.*] Well, I suppose glory must be paid for. [*Exits,* R. D.]

SOLOMON, MARY ANNE, *the cook, and* SOPHIE, *the maid, enter,* C. L. *As the girls come forward they speak.*

Mary Anne and Sophie. [*Together.*] Do you want me, ma'am.

Mrs. W. Sophie, put the spare rooms to rights at once, and be sure to get extra lamps.

Sophie. Yes'm. And may I just go out for a quarter of an hour.

Mrs. W. What for?

Sophie. Only to my sister's to fix up my new dress—when the soldiers come I want to look my best.

Mrs. W. [*Stunned.*] Heavens! [*Aloud.*] Oh, go.

Sophie. Thank you, ma'am. [*Exits*, C. L., *on a run.*]

Mrs. W. That's a country servant for you. [*To Mary.*] Now, let's see about the marketing. [*Goes to table and sits.* MARY *stands by her and consults.*]

WINTHROP *re-enters with check, which he gives his wife.*

Winthrop. Here, my dear, here's the check. Here's your money—five dollars.

Mrs. W. Five dollars! You'll please to put a nought to that.

Win. Oh, well, put it yourself.

Mrs. W. I'll put two. [WIN. *beckons to Sol.*]

Win. Solomon!

Sol. [R.] Yes, sir.

Win. Bring up both wines, you understand.

Sol. [*Going up.*] Yes, sir. I suppose a couple of dozen bottles will do to begin on.

Win. I should hope so. You must take care of their servants, too. Make them comfortable in the kitchen.

Sol. Leave it to me, sir. They won't want to go away for a month. [*Exits*, C. L. WIN. *gets* R.]

Mrs. W. [*Rising—to Mary.*] And two quarters of lamb.

Mary. [*Back of table.*] Lor, mum, soldiers never do care for lamb.

Mrs. W. How do you know?

Mary. Why, mum, I had a young man—I mean a cousin—in the army, and he wouldn't look at lamb. I never dared to offer him nothing but roast beef.

Mrs. W. Be careful not to waste, and don't make any mistakes whatever you do.

Mary. [*Crosses behind to* C.] Bless you, mum, when I cook for the family I may sometimes go a bit wrong, but if I have to cook for the soldiers, I shall cook with all my heart. [*Exits*, C. L.]

Win. [*Looks at watch.*] Isn't it lunch time? I'm frightfully hungry.

Mrs. W. [*Rising.*] Now *don't* annoy me with trifles at such a moment. I've too much to look after.

SOLOMON *re-enters with card,* C. L.

Solomon. Gentleman called sir, and waiting.
Win. [*Reads.*] "Mr. Rothschild, Hoffmeister." Who is he?
Mrs. W. It's the new man that's taken Pellet's drug store.
I suppose he's called to introduce himself. [*Crosses to* R.]
Win. I don't want to know the druggist. [*Nods to* SOL., *who exits,* C. L.]
Mrs. W. You must see him, I have no time. [*Exits rapidly,* R. D.]
Win. [*Following her.*] I've no time, neither.

ROTH *enters, hat in hand,* C. L.

Roth. Good morning. [*He is a fair-haired, spectacled young German, not ridiculous by any means—a slight accent permissible.*]
Win. [*Stays* R.] Ah! How are you?
Roth. Thank you. Will you allow me a few minutes of your most valuable time? Animated by the desire of entering at once into social relations with the families more distinguished of the vicinage, among the inhabitants of which I have the honor now to be enrolled in a capacity quasi professional in character, I have taken the liberty of presenting myself, at the earliest possible moment, to your honored and esteemed self.
Win. [*Sits,* R., *on sofa.*] Yes. [*Aside.*] He's got that speech by heart. [*Aloud.*] Pray be seated.
Roth. [*Sits on edge of chair.*] In addition to the reason already advanced, my visit has an object more personal. I have come most respectfully to a favor solicit.
Win. Ah!

MARY ANNE *appears,* C. L., *with basket on arm, and hat and shawl on.*

Roth. Permit me to make a preliminary statement, in order to give a clearer conception of my motives. [MARY ANNE, *at* L. U. E., *has beckoned to* Win.]
Win. [*Waves her off.*] Get out! [*Subdued tone.*]
Roth. [*Rises.*] I beg pardon—
Win. No, no. Don't mind me. Go on, please.
Roth. [*Sitting on edge of chair.*] My native place—in which I spent the happy days of childhood, reposes on the romantic borders of the Rhine, immediately contiguous to the confluence of the Necker. [MARY ANNE *has beckoned more earnestly.*]
Win. [*Same business.*] No time, now, go away. [MARY ANNE *exits, angrily,* C. L.]

Roth. [*Rises.*] In that case allow me to call at some future—

Win. Excuse me—I spoke to the cook. Please be seated. You were saying—

Roth. [*Sits.*] That I spent the happy days of childhood on the borders of the Rhine, contiguous to the confluence of the Neck—

MRS. WINTHROP *enters,* R. D., *and starts to go back.*

Win. [*Detains her.*] Ah! There is my wife—allow me, my dear—this is Mr. Rhinemeister, from the confluence of the Necker—Mr. Necker—Mr. Hoffmeister—my wife—excuse me— [*As he exits,* R. D., MRS. W. *tries to detain him, catching his coat tail—he breaks away.*]

Roth. Certainly. Don't mind me.

Mrs. Winthrop. [*Aside.*] How provoking. [*They sit.*]

Roth. Madam, animated by the desire of entering at once into social relations with the families most distinguished of the vicinage, among the inhabitants of which I have the honor to be now enrolled in a capacity—

MARY ANNE *enters,* C. L., *as before, and beckons to Mrs. W.*

Mrs. W. [*Rises, and motions her away.*] Not now—by-and-by. [MARY ANNE *exits, in despair.*]

Roth. [*Rising.*] I beg pardon.

Mrs. W. Excuse me, I addressed the cook.

Roth. [*Aside.*] The cook again! So!

MILLY *enters,* R. D.

Mrs. W. [*Rising.*] My dear Millicent, will you kindly represent me for a few moments? [*Introducing.*] Miss Merritt, Mr. Hoffmeister. [*To Roth.*] Pray, pardon me if I attend to some most pressing household duties. [*Calls.*] Mary Anne! [*Exits, after Mary Anne,* C. L.]

Roth. I'm afraid I've dropped in at a bad time.

Mil. [R.] Not at all. It's only a temporary excitement, caused by the unexpected arrival of the soldiers. So you have settled in the place? [*Both sit.*]

Roth. Yes, Miss.

Mil. I hope you will be pleased with it.

TELKA *and* LINDA *appear,* C. L.

Roth. I hope so. And animated by the desire of entering at once into social relations with families most distinguished—

[TELKA *picks up Roth's hat and puts it on.* MIL. *motions her to desist.* ROTH *sees motion and stops.* LINDA *gets down,* R.]

Mil. [*Turns to Roth.*] I beg your pardon—you were saying? Excuse my inattention.

Roth. [*Rises.*] Oh, never mind. I know. It's the cook. [*Turns and sees Telka with his hat on.*] Oh! my gracious, my hat.

Telka. [*Takes off hat, and salutes him.*] The cook is very much obliged, sir. Ha! ha! ha! [*Runs out, with the hat,* C. L.]

Mil. [*Calling.*] Telka!

Roth. Miss! my hat!

Mil. [*Rising.*] I'll get it. [*Calls.*] Telka! [*Exits,* C. L.]

Roth. [*Aside.*] What an extraordinary family! Everybody runs away! [*Turns and sees Linda.*] No—one is left. A nice one.

Linda. [*Aside,* R.] I suppose I must speak. I wonder who he is.

Roth. [*Aside.*] If there is nobody, I must talk to her without an introduction. Animated by the desire, etc.

Linda. } *Together.* { I—eh—
Roth. }   { Eh—I. [*Pause*]

Roth. [*Aside.*] My soda water young lady! [*Aloud.*] I suppose I have the honor of addressing the daughter of the building?

Linda. No. *My* father is Mr. Peregrine Bunker.

Roth. I am glad to hear that. I intended taking the liberty of calling on your father to-day. My name is Rothschild Hoffmeister. I have bought out the apothecary—

Linda. Oh! then please don't call to-day, as we expect to have the house full of soldiers. [*Sits.*] Won't you—be seated.

Roth. [*Smiles and nods, half attempting to sit down, without reaching the chair.*] Just like this family. Animated by the desire—

Linda. Yes. You can imagine how papa's time is taken up. We will probably give a ball. Do you dance?

Roth. Do I dance? I assure you, solemnly, Miss, that when I hear music, I cannot keep still already. [*Sways to and fro, on seat.*]

Linda. Then you'll do lots of business, for we are all crazy about dancing.

Roth. I'd rather dance than eat or sleep any day.

Linda. And I could pass my life in a waltz.

Roth. Oh, Miss, you ought to be German. You are good enough to be.

Linda. Do *you* waltz?

2

Roth. [*Rises.*] That is where my country has the advantage.
I waltz like a top.

Linda. And reverse, too?

Roth. Every way—like a roasting Jack. [LINDA *hums a
waltz; both dance two or three steps, as they face each other they
stop abashed and re-seat themselves.*]

Linda. Then I can promise you, you'll have the entrée everywhere in Narragansett Pier.

Roth. And get all at once acquainted. I'm glad of that. It
is hard to call in on everybody. You have a word that ex-
presses what I look when I do so. I look like a baby—I mean
a booby. Is it not?

Linda. Oh!

Roth. You noticed it?

Linda. No—you don't appear at all awkward now.

Roth. [*Very nervous and uneasy, strikes hand-bell on table
unconsciously, is still more distressed.*] The fact is I am astonishing myself. I never felt so easy. It must be you. You don't
seem the least like a stranger. In fact, I cannot believe we meet
for the first time.

Linda. [*Struck, aside, rises.*] That's exactly like what Telka
spoke about!

Roth. [*Rises.*] It seems as if I had known you forever.

Linda. [*Confused.*] It is very singular, indeed.

Roth. Very singular.

Linda. [*Aside, looks around.*] I wish somebody would come.
I hope he is not going to get the fever. [*Up stage.*]

ROTH *has knocked a book off the table, picks it up with head bent
    down; in this position he dives into* WINTHROP *who enters
    rather quickly; also enter* MRS. WINTHROP, TELKA *and*
    MILLY, C. L.

Winthrop. Where is he? Ah! Mr. Confluence of the Necker,
still here? I hope you'll excuse us—we are so busy to-day.

Roth. Pray, don't mention it. Animated by the desire—

Mrs. Winthrop. The unexpected responsibility of entertaining
the officers of the—

Roth. [C., *bowing on every side.*] Not another word, madam,
sir, I have made my visit already boundless. Permit me to—
[*Bows.*] Animated by the desire—

Win. [R.] Certainly, good-bye.

Mrs. W. [*Smiling mechanically.*] Good day.

Roth. Good day. [*Looks at Linda.*] Oh, she's the nicest
one of them all. [*Bows to Win., going up bumps against Telka
who is up stage talking with Mil.*] Your servant, ladies. [*Bows.*]

Telka. [*Aside to Mil.*] Poor fellow. [*Aloud to him.*] You'll find your hat in the hall.

Roth. Thanks, thanks, thanks, thanks! [*Exits,* C. L.]

Mrs. W. Was anything so provoking. The butcher is actually sold out. Every one was there before us.

Win. [*Gets* R.] Well, we'll give them something else.

Mrs. W. But what?

Win. If the baker isn't sold out, order in a load of pies.

Mrs. W. [*Crosses to* R.] What! I'm at my wit's end. [*Talks to Mil., aside.*]

Win. Perhaps you can borrow some beef. [*Crosses to* C.]

Tel. [C.] Uncle, shall we make up wreaths of flowers and evergreens for the parlor?

Linda. [R.] And put bouquets in the rooms?

Win. [*Crosses between the two girls.*] Flowers! Bouquets! What for?

Tel. [L.] Why, I always read that troops on the march were greatly revived and comforted by having maidens dressed in white come and strew flowers before 'em.

Win. That's only proper on their return from war—not on their way to a Summer encampment.

Linda. What a pity—such a nice idea spoiled.

Tel. Any way we can put flowers in their rooms. [LINDA *joins Telka.*]

Win. As many as you like.

BUNKER *enters,* C. L.

Bunker. Just think, Winthrop, I can't find a place to put eleven—

Win. Now look here, Bunker, I've had enough of this business.

Bun. My friend, I'm surprised at you.

Win. Just reflect a little! Here are my wife, my niece and her companion. Three ladies against four officers.

Bun. I never thought of that. The fourth officer will find it rather dull. [*Laughs.*]

Win. I'm not jesting. The more I think of it, the more annoyed I feel.

Bun. [*Struck.*] Is that so? Well, perhaps I can arrange it. I've just heard that there's sudden sickness at Ruggle's house, where the Colonel was going to stop. If you'll take him I'll put the lieutenants somewhere else.

Win. [*Struck.*] The Colonel! An elderly person, of course —with pleasure.

Tel. [*Grieved, crosses to Win.*] Oh, uncle! A nasty old colonel.

Mrs. W. [*Down* R.] I object for one. He will require too much attention.

Tel. An old fussy growler! We won't be jolly a bit!

Win. [*Severely.*] Jolly! My house is not a place of amusement. [*To Bun.*] I accept the Colonel.

Bun. Then we must see about it at once. Come with me—the quartermasters have just got off the train. The regiment's coming up on the boat.

Win. Come along. Where's my hat and coat?

Mrs. W. But, my dear—

Win. I have fully considered. I take the Colonel or nobody. [*Exits,* R. D.]

Mrs. W. I don't know whether I'm standing on my feet or not. [*Exits, following Win.,* R. D.]

Linda. [*Seizes Bun*] No Colonel for us, papa. [*Warmly.*]

Bun. No dear—we have the surgeon. [*Takes out card.*]

Linda. [*Takes billet dubiously.*] A doctor? Let's see. [*Stage* L.]

WINTHROP *re-enters.*

Winthrop. Now then, Bunker! Don't lose a moment, we must secure that Colonel. [*They exit,* C. L.]

Linda. [*Reads billet.*] "Dolf Van Tassel, M.D."

Mil. [*Startled.*] Oh, my! My husband.

Linda. What's the matter? [*Crosses to Mil.*]

Mil. [R., *controls herself.*] Nothing.

Tel. [*Turns up her nose.*] A doctor! That's a nice one to have.

Mil. A doctor may be a very amiable person.

SOLOMON *enters,* C. L.

Solomon. Officer called and waiting.

Tel. and Linda. An officer! [*Rapturously embracing.*]

Sol. I think he's going to be quartered here, Miss; he looked me all over.

Tel. [*Impatiently.*] Show him in at once. [SOL. *exits,* C. L.]

Mil. I'll call Mrs. Winthrop. [*Exits,* R. D.]

Tel. [*Runs to mirror over mantel.*] Is my hair tumbled? [*Fixes it.*]

Linda. [*Puts on her hat.*] I look best in a hat. [*Runs to mirror at other side and fixes it.*]

Tel. I'm a perfect fright.

Linda. [*Adjusting hat.*] I was going home anyway.

THORPE SYDAM *enters,* C. L., *looks about; sees no one; puts helmet on table and goes to glass at* C., *takes out two brushes and carefully does his hair. Wears captain's uniform.*

Tel. [*Turns.*] How red my hands are. [*Raises them above her head, waves them to make them white.*]

Linda. [*Pulling on gloves.*] The very worst pair of gloves I've got—a whole number too big. [*Turns and sees Syd. To Tel.*] There he is!

Tel. Where? [*Sees him, snatches up book and throws herself in chair, feigning to read.* LINDA *pretends to busy herself at piano.*]

Sydam. [C., *having finished, puts up brushes, sticks glass in eye, takes up helmet and comes slowly down stage; sees ladies.*] Haw! Here's one young lady, and there's another. [*Produces flacon and perfumes himself.*] Beg pardon, ladies, if I intrude, but the occasion. Permit me to introduce myself—Thorpe Sydam of the Excelsior Regiment, N. G. S. N. Y.

Tel. [*Rises.*] My name is Telka Essoff. [*Introduces.*] My friend, Miss Linda Bunker.

Syd. Many thanks.

Tel. Please be seated ; my aunt will be here directly.

Syd. [C.] Your aunt? Oh, there's no hurry. [*All sit.*] I perceive I interrupted your reading.

Tel. Yes; I was so absorbed I didn't notice your entrance.

Linda. We didn't even see you come in.

Syd. Must be a very fascinating book.

Linda. Do you like reading?

Syd. Yes, oh, yes. I never have time to read myself, but some of the boys do, and they tell the rest of us about it. It's all the same among the boys who reads, you know.

MRS. WINTHROP *enters,* R. D., SYD. *rises and* TEL. *introduces.* LINDA *crosses to table.*

Tel. My aunt.

Syd. [*Bows.*] I am Thorpe Sydam of the Excelsior Regiment, N. G. S. N. Y.

Mrs. Winthrop. I suppose you called about the officers' quarters.

Syd. Yes. Pardon me for causing inconvenience

Mrs. W. Don't mention it. I hear that four officers are coming.

Syd. Yes. Four of ours. I suppose it's my duty to inspect the premises according to army regulations; but one glance at the ladies is sufficient to assure me of the welcome of the four. I really envy them, but it's all the same among the boys; if one of the boys is in luck, the other boys are. All the same among the boys, no matter which of the boys is in luck, you know.

Mrs. W. You are very kind. The gentlemen will have to make some allowance for the shortness of our notice.

Syd. Yes. That's the new system, you know. Everything on short notice. So we'll be always prepared. The boys don't mind it, but I'm afraid you may.

Mrs. W. How long do you intend to remain in our place?

Syd. Too short a time to suit your guests. Not over a day— we are due in Newport to-morrow evening.

Tel. [*Who, with Linda, has been feverishly attentive to all Syd. says, checks off his words with smiles; crosses to* L. C.] That's very reasonable, aunty, you must admit.

Linda. We hope to see the review to-morrow.

Syd. Ya'as. It'll be very good. The boys are to have a sham battle and all that. It'll be quite a topper.

Tel. [*Crosses to Mrs. W.*] Aunt, we *must* drive out and see it.

Syd. Charming. The boys will be sure to conquer under your eyes.

WINTHROP *enters,* C. L., *sees group.*

Winthrop. [*Aside.*] One of the warriors here already.

Mrs. W. [*Rises.*] My dear, this gentleman has come about the quarters.

Win. [C.] Delighted to meet you. I've just come from the quartermaster himself where I solicited the pleasure of entertaining your Colonel. [*With emphasis.*]

Mrs. W. Humph!

Tel. Oh! [*Petulantly turns up stage,* L.]

Syd. The Colonel will arrive with the regiment.

Win. So I understand. The four young gentlemen allotted to me will be quartered at the neighboring brewery.

Syd. At the brewery! That'll be jolly. The boys will like that.

Tel. [*Crosses to Win.*] But, uncle, even if you take the Colonel, we could keep some lieutenants, too.

Win. [*Gives her threatening look; she gets back.*] We'll give the brewery a chance.

Syd. [*Aside,* L. C.] Deuced charming little thing. I don't believe the brewery comes up to this. [*Aloud.*] As my business is unhappily concluded, allow me to take my leave.

Mrs. W. [*Crosses to Syd.*] Won't you take lunch with us? I've just ordered it.

Syd. Madam, this is really too kind. [MILITARY MUSIC—*a march heard in distance.*]

Win. You must stay. [*Rings,* L., *table.*]

Tel. Hark! [*Listens; hears music in distance.*]

SOPHIE *rushing in,* C. L.

Sophie. They're coming! They're coming!

Mrs. W. What is it?

Sophie. The soldiers! [MUSIC *louder.*]

Win. Already?

Tel. [*Very quickly.*] Will they pass by our house? [*Runs to window at side.*]

Syd. Certainly!

MILLY *runs in,* R. D.

Milly. Let me see too! Let me see too!

Tel. [*Speaking back into room.*] Here comes the band! [MRS. W. *goes to window,* L. U. E.]

Mary and Sophie. There they are. There they are.

SOLOMON *enters with tray, bottles and glasses,* C. L.

Solomon. Here's the music for you.

Syd. How they love the military.

Mrs. W. [*Shoves up the window, and the full burst of music comes in with the distant shouts.*] There!

MARY ANNE *runs in,* C. L., *with tray of luncheon and tea service and runs with it to window.* SOL. *goes with his tray to Syd.* TEL. *crosses to Syd. and back to window.* LINDA *runs up* C., *spins Win. round.* MRS. W. *runs to Win. and pulls him to window. Tableau of excitement to military march.*

All. [*As curtain comes down.*] Look at 'em! Look at 'em!

CURTAIN.

ACT II.

SCENE—*Same as Act First. March continues. Curtain rises immediately and finds* SOLOMON *and* SOPHIE *in place.* SOLO-MON, R., *winding clock.*

Sophie. Solomon! Solomon!
Solomon. [*Not turning round.*] Well, what is it?
Sophie. Here he is again.
Sol. Who?
Sophie. The other young officer that asked after the colonel. He wants to know if he's come yet.
Sol. [*Coming down.*] No, he ain't come yet.
Sophie. I thought not. [*Exits,* C. L.]
Sol. That's the sixth time to-day he's come to ask after the colonel. Why, he's coming in.

DOLF VAN TASSEL, M.D., *enters,* C. L., *Surgeon of regiment.*

Dolf. Sh! [*Puts finger to his lips.*]
Sol. [R.] The colonel ain't come yet.
Dolf. Thanks for the information. [*Gives money.*]
Sol. Thank *you,* sir.
Dolf. It's very unfortunate that I can't find the colonel. I've called I believe—
Sol. Six times, sir.
Dolf. [L.] Yes, and my quarters are at the other end of the town, at Mr. Peregrine Bunker's house.
Sol. Can't you wait for the colonel here, sir?
Dolf. [*Quickly.*] Can I? At least, would there be no objection to my stopping?
Sol. Not the least, sir. I'll tell Mr. Winthrop.
Dolf. Do. [*Gives money.*] You are very good.
Sol. *You* are very good, sir. [*Going,* R., *aside.*] If they all come down like this I'll make my fortune before the regiment leaves town. [*Exits,* R. D.]
Dolf. I'm in the house. If I could get word to Milly. [*Looks round.*]

MILLY *enters cautiously,* L. D.

Milly. Dolf!
Dolf. [*Puts helmet on table,* R., *and embraces her.*] My darling!

Mil. [L.] I saw you from the window.

Dolf. I've been here six times.

Mil. I saw you every time.

Dolf. If I.could have got only one glimpse of you.

Mil. You know how careful I must be.

Dolf. [*Sighs.*] Yes.

Mil. If any one in the house suspected our—

Dolf. Our happiness. [*Kisses her.*]

Mil. [*Disengaging, crosses to* R.] Do be reasonable.

Dolf. Certainly. [*Kisses her.*]

Mil. [*Disengaging and turning to* R.] Let us begin to arrange how we can see each other.

Dolf. Pleasure first, business afterwards.

Mil. Some one will see us.

Telka. [*Outside,* C. L.] Milly. [*They separate.*]

Mil. [R.] There, our opportunity is gone and we've settled nothing.

TELKA *enters, taking off hat,* C. L.

Telka. I've just driven by the brewery. Our four officers are there.

Mil. [*Remonstrating, points to Dolf.*] Telka. [*Crosses to* C.]

Tel. [*To Mil.*] Ah, the doctor! [*Nodding to him.*] How do you do again? [*To Mil.*] I became acquainted with him when he called before. [*To Dolf.*] It's so nice of you to come over again.

Dolf. No thanks. It's my duty. [*Aside to Mil.,* L.] Send her away.

Mil. [*Aside to him.*] That would never do.

Tel. [*To Mil.*] Has the new music come?

Mil. Yes. You'll find it on the piano.

Tel. [*Goes to piano.*] I wonder if my Russian songs are here? [DOLF *kisses Mil.'s hand.*]

Mil. Do be careful.

Dolf. I will. [*Squeezes hand in both of his.*]

Tel. [*After rummaging.*] Here it is. [*Turns and catches Dolf's motions.*] What are you about?

Mil. Oh. [*Trying to withdraw her hand.*]

Dolf. [*Counting her pulse.*] Five, six, seven, eight! Yes, as I told you before, you ought to do something for it.

Tel. Are you sick, Milly?

Dolf. She won't acknowledge it, but I perceived it at once. Heart! [*Taps his chest. Crosses to* C.]

Tel. Dear me!

Dolf. [*Goes to table and sits.*] I'll give you a prescription.

Tel. [*To Mil.*] Why didn't you speak to the little new apothecary when he was here this morning?

Mil. [L.] The fact is, I have no confidence in him.

Tel. And you never complained?

Mil. Because I'm ashamed to speak to any one about my heart.

Dolf. [*Approaches with paper.*] Be sure you follow the directions.

Tel. Let's see. [*Crosses to* C. MIL. *holds the paper away.*] I'm so worried. [*To Dolf.*] Is there any danger? [MIL. *gets* L.]

Dolf. Oh, no—not for the present. [*They converse.*]

Mil. [*Reads—aside.*] As soon as the colonel arrives, I can call again. You understand. [*Aloud.*] I am very much obliged, doctor.

Dolf. No thanks. It's my duty.

MR. *and* MRS. WINTHROP *enter*, R. D.

Winthrop. Good morning again, Doctor.

Dolf. [*Shaking hands warmly.*] Good morning.

Mrs. Winthrop. We're waiting like yourself for the colonel. [*Crosses and speaks to* MIL., *who exits into garden*, R. U. E.]

Win. [*To Dolf.*] You are very anxious to see him?

Dolf. [*Going to look after Mil.*] The very first thing. It's my duty.

Win. I hope there's no sickness in the case.

Dolf. [*Looking after Mil.*] Oh. Just a trifle.

Win. A touch of gout, eh?

Dolf. [*Slowly and absently.*] Eh! Oh!

Win. [R.] I feel it, too. Comes from the liver.

Dolf. [*Takes helmet.*] Yes—the liver—oh, yes. I wish you a very good day.

Win. Don't hurry.

Dolf. Thanks, I must. [*Going.*] It's my duty.

Win. [*Confidentially taking his arm.*] How about the colonel's diet. Nothing special required, eh?

Dolf. [*Going up with him.*] Oh, no.

Win. But nothing greasy—no acids, of course.

Dolf. [C. L.] Of course. Good day. [*Exits, after bowing to ladies,* C. L.]

Mrs. W. Good day, doctor.

Tel. [L.] Well, if the colonel don't come soon, he may stay away, for all I care.

Mrs. W. [*Reproachfully.*] Telka!

Win. [*Severe, seated.*] Be careful how you talk in his presence. Remember his age.

Telka. [*Sighs.*] I do. More's the pity.

Win. You must pay him every attention.

Tel. [*Sits on sofa.*] I'll do my best. I'll give him all I intended for our young lieutenants.

Win. [*To Mrs. W.*] Is everything ready, dear.

Mrs. W. Yes; we'll put him in the corner room.

Win. That's a good idea. There's a stove in it.

Mrs. W. A stove! In August?

Win. The evenings are chilly, and for an old man with the gout— [*Sees Solomon.*]

SOLOMON *enters,* R. D., *to go to* C. L.

Win. Solomon, have the stove in the corner room ready to light.

Solomon. Yes, sir. [*Exits,* C. L.]

Mrs. W. [*Sarcastically.*] We might bring down grandpa's roller chair from the garret, and make a hospital of the house— with the tea-kettle simmering all day.

Win. I'd rather get hot tea for the old colonel, than have to apply ice to the brains of young love-struck lieutenants.

Tel. [*Crosses to* C., *and up.*] I don't know what the lieutenants have ever done to you.

Mrs. W. Nor I.

Win. [*Sarcastic.*] How nice it would be to have the rascals kissing the fair hands of the lady of the house. [*Mrs. W. goes to him as if to reproach him.*] And courting the niece. But a sickly old colonel won't do it. He's got something else to think of.

Tel. [*At window.*] Oh, look at that lovely officer galloping down the road.

Mrs. W. [*Eagerly running to window.*] Oh, where?

Win. The young devils are galloping all over town. And every girl's heart is galloping after them.

Tel. He's stopping at our door.

Win. The adjutant, I suppose, come to announce—

Tel. See how he leaps off his horse.

Mrs. W. The adjutant, of course.

Tel. [*Comes away.*] I hope he's got to stop where the colonel does.

SOLOMON *admits the* COLONEL, C. L. *He is young and dashing.*

Colonel. [*Cheerfully.*] Good day!

Win. [R.] You have come to announce the Colonel, I suppose. Is he coming?

Col. [C.] He begs your pardon for announcing himself so abruptly. I am the Colonel—Colonel Van Kleck.

Mrs. W. and Tel. [L.] Oh!

Win. [*Dumb.*] You—are—the Colonel?

Col. May I ask to be presented to the ladies?

Win. Ye—yes. Oh, yes—certainly. My wife—and my niece.

Tel. [L., *aside to Mrs. W.*] He doesn't look his age, aunty.

Mrs. W. [*Aside to Tel.*] I don't believe he has the gout, either.

Win. [*Aside.*] Why, he's as young as any of 'em.

Mrs. W. Our house is yours, Colonel. If there is anything you wish—

Col. My only wish is to cause as little trouble as possible. I shall be pained if the hospitality you extend to us is productive of the slightest inconvenience.

Mrs. W. [*Shakes hands, earnestly.*] We bid you a most hearty welcome. [*Crosses to Win.*]

Win. [R., *resignedly.*] Make yourself completely at home. Telka!

Tel. [*To Col.*] May I take your helmet, sir?

Col. Certainly not. [*Crosses and gives helmet quickly to* SOL., *who exits,* L. D., *and then returns;* COL. *unbuckles sword and gives that to* SOL., *who exits,* C.] But if you will give me your hand in welcome, I shall take it with thanks. [WIN. *and* MRS. W. *converse.*]

Tel. [*Shakes hands.*] Willingly! There it is. But I have to make you an apology.

Col. [L.] An apology? Why?

Tel. I've been calling you an old gentleman and thinking all sorts of ugly *old* things about you.

Col. Is that all? I forgive if you tell me how you came to do it.

Tel. [*Goes to Mrs. W.*] I'll tell you—when we become better acquainted. [*Exits with* MRS. W., R. U. E.; *as she goes off,* MRS. W. *kisses her hand at the* Col., *who does not percieve it.* WIN. *runs up stage, looks surprised and amazed.*]

Win. [*To Col.*] Will you have a light luncheon sent to your room, Colonel, or would you prefer to lie down a little first.

Col. [*A little surprised.*] Oh, no. I've only been two hours on horseback. I'm quite fresh.

Win. [*Closes window,* L. U. E.] I'll shut out the draught.

Col. [R.] I don't mind it; but if it's disagreeable to you—

Win. You should mind it. You'll find the weather-strips are on all your windows.

Col. You are very good. I always sleep with my windows open.

Win. Windows open?

Col. Winter and summer.

Win. [*Aside.*] He won't acknowledge his infirmities. [*Aloud.*] If you have any special orders for our cook, don't stand on ceremony.

Col. You are too good. I don't think of anything.

Win. You *must* be careful of your diet.

Col. [R.] I? I could eat pebbles when I'm hungry.

Win. [*Aside.*] Mere bravado. [*Aloud, knowingly.*] Leave it to me. I'll see you don't have anything too rich.

Col. Too rich?

Win. It would be poison in your condition.

Col. My condition? What condition?

Win. Why, your liver complaint and gout, of course.

Col. My dear sir, I noticed it before—you seem to take me for an invalid.

Win. [*Apologetically.*] Not at all. I understand—we, none of us, like to acknowledge—but I learned of it quite by accident.

Col. Learned of it from whom, pray?

Win. [*Nods confidentially.*] The regimental surgeon hinted at the state of your case.

Col. What could have possessed him!

Win. He is very much concerned. He's been here six times already.

Col. When he calls for the seventh time, I will take the liberty of reassuring him. [*Crosses to* L.]

Win. I trust you are not vexed with us.

Col. [*Amazed.*] Not at all. I enjoy the joke. Your solicitude is explained.

Win. Ha! ha! ha! Yes, my wife suggested a warming-pan.

Col. [*Not so much amused.*] Warming-pan! Very thoughtful of her.

Roll of drum and color-march heard. This is continued till soldiers are off.

Win. [*Starts.*] What's that?

Col. [*Going up.*] They are bringing me the colors.

Win. [*Following.*] Let me show you your room.

Col. I beg you won't trouble yourself. [*Exits,* L. D.]
Win. He *is* mad.

TELKA *enters,* R. U. E.

Telka. Uncle, there's a lot of soldiers coming in; what on earth is the matter?
Win. [*Gravely.*] Nothing, child. They are only bringing in the colors.

Guards cross stage, C. L., *exeunt,* R. U. E. *They do* NOT *keep step.* SOL. *remains.*

Tel. [*Holding Win.'s arm.*] Oh, uncle. There's a lieutenant.
Win. What of it?
Tel. Can't we ask him to dinner?
Win. Certainly not.

PAUL DEXTER *enters,* C. L., *and speaks to* SOL., *who is just going to follow guards out.*

Tel. [*Excited,* R.] There's another!
Win. So there is! They spring up like mushrooms!
Tel. Isn't he splendid!
Win. [*Takes her to door.*] You had better go and see if your aunt wants you.
Tel. I declare, it's too bad, I'm not to have the least bit of comfort with the soldiers. [*Exits,* R. D. *Soldiers return and exeunt,* C.]
Sol. [*To Paul.*] I can't say, but here's Mr. Winthrop.
Paul. [*Helmet in hand.*] My name is Paul Dexter. I have the pleasure of being quartered here.
Win. There is a slight error. We have the honor of entertaining the Colonel. You perceive my list. [*Shows paper.*]
Paul. [*Glances at it.*] Correct. Colonel Van Kleck and staff.
Win. [*Looking.*] And staff?
Paul. Yes. The colonel, lieutenant-colonel, major, adjutant, quartermaster and medical officers. I'm the adjutant.
Win. [R., *dryly.*] I shall have quite a family.
Paul. Sorry to trouble you, of course, but—
Win. [*Rises.*] Oh, I'm delighted. I'll go tell my wife. Excuse me just a moment.
Paul. Certainly.

Win. [*Going, aside.*] A young colonel and a dozen young staves. It's perfectly lovely. [*Exits,* R. D.]

Paul. They don't appear to receive us with joy. [*To Sol.*] I say, old friend, I've been several hours on horseback, and should like to retire to my room, if not inconvenient.

Sol. I'll see to it at once, sir. [*Exits,* L. D.]

SYDAM *enters,* C. L.

Sydam. Hollo, old boy!

Paul. [R.] Hollo! You here?

Syd. [*Brushing his back hair at mantel.*] Yes. Saw you come up, and came to congratulate you on the quarters. I know the family. Nice people. One of the young ladies is—well—she's—what shall I call her?

Paul. Take your own time and consider. [*On sofa,* R.]

Syd. [*At fireplace,* L.] Quite a topper. But she don't belong here. I mean she's from abroad. Prussian—no—not that—

Paul. Russian?

Syd. That's it. None of your shallow, blasé, languid sort, but thoroughbred—full of fire—eyes like a gazelle.

Paul. Like a what?

Syd. [L.] I guess it's a gazelle. But I never saw one. That's what the poets say.

Paul. My son, you are much damaged. Poetry! It's a dreadful attack.

Syd. I'm afraid I shall gush about her. ·But business, old boy. I'm going to work to get up a ball; I hope the Colonel won't object.

Paul. I'll ask him.

Syd. Do. I'll call again before dinner, to hear what he says.

Paul. And to see the little Russian.

Syd. [*Pleased.*] How the deuce did you guess it! The fact is, I'm quite gone, I acknowledge. Very inconvenient, too. If she was only in Newport, where we camp a week. But here, where we only stop a day—

Paul. Oh, you're used to it. This is your fifth in a year.

Syd. Yes; but the others were nothing. I'm done for this time.

Paul. Are you serious? Pardon my joking.

Syd. That's all right—among the boys, you know.

SCIPIO *enters,* C. L.—*colored military servant.*

Scipio. Please, sir, where shall I put the things?
Paul. I wish I knew, Scipio. Are the horses cared for?
Scip. [C.] Yes, sah. There wasn't no room, but I soon made some.
Paul. How did you manage?
Scip. There was two little ponies in the stable, so I just turned 'em loose.
Paul. Loose! Where?
Scip. In de garden. Golly, dey jumped like lambs.
Paul. The devil!
Syd. [R.] You'll become quite a favorite in the house.
Scip. I guess we is already. Dey fixed me in a room right off de kitchem. Um!

SOLOMON *enters,* L. D.

Solomon. Room's ready, sir.
Paul. [*To Scip.*] In there, you rascal. [SCIP. *exits,* L. D.] Now, to brush the dust off.
Syd. If you don't mind, I'll take your brush a minute, too.
Paul. With pleasure. Walk in. [*Holds door for him.*]
Syd. After you.
Paul. I'm at home.
Syd. All the same among the boys, you know, who goes first. [*Exeunt,* L. D.]
Sol. Now, we've got a house full.

TELKA *enters,* R. U. E., *excited, followed by* MILLY.

Telka. Solomon, I've just caught my ponies running loose over the flower-beds. Who turned them out?
Sol. [L.] The officer's servant, Miss.
Tel. [*Angrily.*] The Colonel's?
Sol. No, Miss, the Lieutenant's.
Tel. [*Mollified.*] Very well. Don't tell my uncle, it might vex him. [*Turns towards piano.*]
Sol. All right, Miss. [*Goes up and arranges furniture.*]
Milly. [R., *at piano.*] You had better get your music out, Telka. Remember, your uncle will certainly ask you to sing after dinner.
Tel. Oh, dear; have I got to sit and sing instead of talking. [*Goes to piano.*]

Scipio *re-enters,* L. D., *looks at the door and makes a large chalk X on it.*

Sol. Here, what are you doing? What's that for?

Scipio. Make no mistake 'bout de door. [*Crosses to* C.]

Sol. It's a fine invention. Is it your own idea?

Scip. Yes, sah. Invented it all out of my own head.

Sol. How clever! I'm afraid you'll die early. [*Exits,* C. L.]

Mil. [*To Tel.*] Why not give them a German ballad?

Tel. I havn't learnt any.

SYDAM *and* PAUL *enter,* L. D.

Sydam. [*Stops, to Paul.*] Here they are!

Paul. Introduce me at once.

Tel. Isn't it pretty! I'll try it. [*Sits at piano and sees the officers.*]

Syd. Permit me to present Mr. Paul Dexter.

Tel. [*Rises, sees Paul, clutches Mil., excitedly.*]

Paul. [L.] I am delighted, ladies.

Tel. [*Aside to Mil.*] It's the boarding-school brother!

Syd. I hope we are not in the way.

Tel. [*Timidly,* R. C.] Oh, not at all.

Paul. [*To Tel., crossing to her.*] You were about to sing?

Tel. No. I don't know the accompaniment.

Paul. If you will permit me, I'll try to become a useful member of the family. May I look at the score? My limited accomplishment may be of service.

Tel. [*Hands music.*] Oh, if you please. [PAUL *crosses to piano.*]

Syd. I'll help, too. I'll turn the leaves. [*Goes to piano.*]

Tel. [*Aside to Mil., impetuously.*] It's Paul!

Mil. Are you sure?

Tel. Didn't you notice that he recognized me at once?

Mil. To be candid, I did not.

Tel. I am sure of it. I *feel* it. [*Hand on heart.*]

Mil. I hope you are not mistaken.

Tel. I'll prove it to you. Mr. Dexter!

Mil. [*Restraining her.*] Telka!

Tel. Let me alone.

Paul. [*Comes down,* R. C.] At your service.

Tel. Were you not at Madam Storrs' boarding-school last year to take your sister home?

Paul. [R.] Yes.

3

Tel. [c., *aside to Mil.*] You see. [*To Paul.*] Do you recall anything particular connected with the visit?

Paul. No. Not that I remember.

Mil. [L., *aside to Tel.*] Now, you see.

Tel. [*Aside to Mil.*] Well, now, you wait. [*To Paul.*] No special recollection of any persons you met there.

Paul. [*Thinking.*] No. Yes! [*Suddenly.*]

Tel. [*Triumphant.*] Go on.

Paul. I shall never forget the short, fat, lady teacher with a moustache and no eyebrows.

Mil. [*Aside to the petrified Tel.*] That wasn't you.

Tel. [*To Mil.*] Of course not. [*To Paul.*] And you noticed no one else?

Paul. Oh, there was a whole flock of young geese.

Mil. [*Aside to Tel.*] You were one of them.

Paul. They all looked alike.

Tel. Of course. [*Crosses to* L. H. PAUL *goes to piano.*]

Mil. [*Same.*] Are you satisfied now?

Tel. [*Stage,* L.] It's an outrage. [*Stamps her foot.*]

Paul. [*At piano.*] Now, if you are ready.

Tel. Thank you, I won't sing.

Paul. What?

Tel. I've changed my mind.

Mil. [*Aside to her.*] Control yourself.

Paul. What's the matter?

Syd. [*Comes down with music.*] By Jove, here's a part exactly like the march I composed.

Tel. [*Meeting him,* c., *very sweetly.* MIL. *gets to sofa, and* PAUL *joins her.*] Indeed, are you a composer, Lieutenant?

Syd. Well, somewhat. I'm sorry you won't sing, though. I'd like to hear a Russian song.

Tel. Have you ever been in my country?

Syd. No—but from what I know of it [*bows*]—it must be—as far as the fair sex is concerned—a—ah—quite a topper.

Tel. As for its women, I warn you to be on your guard. We are vindictive, and *never* forgive or forget an insult. [*Up with Syd.*]

Paul. [*To Mil.*] Is it possible I've given her offense?

Mil. Oh no, she is merely—somewhat spoiled.

Paul. [*Aside.*] So it would seem. [*They sit and talk.*]

WINTHROP *enters,* R. D., *observes group.*

Winthrop. Making themselves at home. The fun is just going to begin. [*Aloud.*] Telka, my dear, your aunt wishes to see you. [*All rise.*]

Tel. [*Heated and looking at Paul.*] Uncle, did you see my ponies in the garden? Some one turned them out, and they have trampled on all the flowers.

Win. [*Sharply.*] Who did it?

Tel. [*With glance at Paul.*] I don't know *who* could have had so little manners, or so little sense. [*Exits quickly*, R. D.]

DOLF *enters,* C. L., PAUL *and* SYD. *go to him and shake hands.*

Win. [*Getting to* L.] There's another! My house is a regular barracks. The Colonel draws the whole regiment after him. I got myself out of the frying-pan into the fire.

Syd. [*Going.*] Bye-bye, old boy, bye-bye; you're in luck. All the same among the boys, though. Good day. [*To* Win.]

Win. [*Short.*] Good day. [PAUL *and* SYD. *exeunt, arm in arm,* C. L.]

Dolf. [R.] So the Colonel has arrived at last?

Win. [*Looking over papers at table,* L.] Yes. He wants you particularly.

Dolf. [*Aside.*] Wants me particularly. Perhaps he's going to announce my appointment to the hospital! Oh, for that unattainable post with the big salary. I've been trying all means for a year to get it. We could keep house on that. [*Aloud.*] Did he seem particularly pleasant?

Win. Very. I think he's got something for you. He's in his room now. [*Points.*] There. [*Goes up.*]

Dolf. [*Who has exchanged signs with* MIL., *kisses his hand to her, the sound causes* WIN. *to turn round, just as* MIL. *strikes a loud chord to attract his attention. To* Win.] Thanks. It's my duty. [*Bows and exits,* L. D. WIN. *goes up to see if all are gone.*]

Mil. [*At piano, playing.*] If I could only contrive to remain here until he comes out.

Win [*Returns.*] Miss Merritt, I warned you before that I do *not* want my niece to be thrown into the society of these young officers.

Mil. [R.] She was only going to sing, sir.

Win. If the gentlemen want music let them sing to each other.

Mil. They just happened in.

Win. No matter. Please see that it don't happen again. [*Exits,* R. U. E.]

Mil. Thank goodness he's gone without sending me away. Now I can have a moment to myself without interruption. [*Sits at piano.*]

DOLF *enters,* L. D., *depressed.*

Dolf. Milly!

Mil. Dolf! What is the matter? How you look!

Dolf. I look like a surgeon who's been dissected, don't I?

Mil. What have you been doing?

Dolf. [L] Listening to the Colonel. He has just opened on me like a madman. After some incoherent ravings about poisoned livers and warming-pans, he ended with an explosion of rage that literally blew me out of the room.

Mil. My poor Dolf.

Dolf. The worst of it is that I shan't dare to call here again.

Mil. [*Determined.*] Then we'll meet somewhere else.

Dolf. We'll have to think of some place.

Mil. How dismal it is to love in secret!

Dolf. Patience, my darling.

Mil. If you knew how I suffer in this false position.

Dolf. [*Takes her in his arms.*] *This* is not a false position. [*Kisses her.*]

Mil. There you go again, tempting fate. We shall be discovered.

COLONEL *appears,* L. D.

Dolf. I'm desperate. I don't care who sees us.

Colonel. [*Advancing.*] So it appears. [*Movement of embarrassment.* MIL. *crosses to* R.] Will you excuse us, Miss? [*To Mil.*] I have some business with this gentleman. [MIL. *hesitates.*] Providing, of course, *you* have nothing more to say to him. [*Crosses to* L.]

Mil. [*Confused.*] I—certainly not.

Col. [*Crosses to her and offers his arm.*] Permit me the honor. [*Conducts her to door—bows.*]

Mil. [*Aside.*] We are both ruined. [*Exits,* R. D.]

Col. [*Buttons coat and turns to Dolf.*] Ahem!

Dolf. [*Aside.*] He buttons up his coat. This is official.

Col. [*After striding up and down.*] Doctor, I am at a loss for words to characterize your behavior.

Dolf. [*Aside.*] I bet he finds some in a moment.

Col. First, you make me ridiculous in the family with your gout, and your warming-pans and stuff, and now I find you in a compromising situation with this young person.

Dolf. [*Eagerly.*] The young lady—

Col. The young lady is a member of the family whose hospitality I enjoy. If you have no scruples on your own account and hers, I insist that you exhibit some for me.

Dolf. [*Cooler.*] May I be permitted to explain?

Col. Your behavior cannot be explained. Have a care, sir. You are not only disgracing the uniform you wear, which has never covered any but honorable men. [DOLF *makes a gesture.*] I have not done; but you have your future, which, outside of our regimental connection, I had the power to advance. [DOLF *makes a movement.*] Hear me out. No man, soldier or civilian, has the right to trifle with a woman's good name. [DOLF *begins to smile quietly.*] The creature who steals into a girl's confidence, and, either from frivolity or baseness of heart, pretends a passion he has affected to other victims and intends to simulate to many more, is not fit to—[DOLF *shakes with laughter.*] I see you are moved. If I am wrong—if your intentions to this young lady are honorable—answer me frankly. Do you intend to marry her?

Dolf. No, sir. I do not.

Col. Well, by Jove! [*Stage* R.] Is it possible?

Dolf. Yes. She's my wife.

Col. [*Softer.*] I hope you are not playing another practical joke [*Stage* R.] on me. By Gad, sir, no more warming-pans.

Dolf. [*Running to him, warmly clasps his hand.*] Fred, old fellow, we were friends at school and friends afterwards, and will be, I hope, till we die; yet, in spite of your big fortune and my no fortune, let's cut dignity for a moment, while I make a confidence you'll regard as sacred. I'm married to Milly—I loved her to the verge of desperation. We've concealed our marriage because we are both as poor as a pair of foundlings. I've been waiting for that place you are trying to get for me through your father—and until I got it, or something, I never meant to tell of my folly.

Col. Folly? It isn't folly. By Jove, sir, she's perfectly lovely. If I had been in your place I'd have married her in spite of everything.

Dolf. Would you? Well, if I were in yours, I'd move heaven and earth to help you along.

Col. [*Grasps his hand.*] Would you? I'll do it—trust to me. I'll get you a hospital, if I have to build one. [*Crosses to* L.]

TELKA *and* MILLY *enter,* R. D., PAUL, MRS. WINTHROP *and* WINTHROP *enter,* R. U. E., SOLOMON *enters at back,* C. L.

Dolf. [*Aside, to Col.*] Do me one favor to begin now. Take my wife in to dinner.

Col. With pleasure.

Solomon. Dinner is served. [DOLF *and* PAUL *go to Tel. and offer their arms.*]

Paul. [*To Tel.*] May I— [TEL. *gives her arm to Dolf, and they exeunt,* C. L.]

Col. [*To Mil.*] Ahem! may I— [*Going up stage with her.*] I know everything, I congratulate you. [*Exeunt,* C. L.]

Winthrop. [*To Mrs. W.*] Why didn't you take the Colonel's arm?

Mrs. Winthrop. Because I prefer the lieutenant. [*Takes Paul's arm, and exeunt,* C. L.]

Win. [*Throwing up his hands.*] My wife's gone, too. [*Stage* R.] The lieutenants have captured even her. [*Goes off after crowd,* C. L.]

CURTAIN.

ACT III.

SCENE.—*Room in Bunker's. Doors* R., L. *and* C. *Window* L. *Piano and large screen near Mantel-piece. Table* R. C. *with chairs.*

ROTH *enters,* L. U. E., *trying to detain* JANE.

Roth. But if you please—

Jane. I can't stop a minute.

Roth. But I only want to ask—

Jane. No time to answer questions. The soldiers are waiting for dinner. [*Exits,* R. 1 E.]

Roth. It's the same here as at the other houses, nobody hasn't got no time. They said he was at home, but I don't see anybody.

DOLF *enters,* C. R., *quickly.*

Dolf. Who's there? What, you again, old fellow?

Roth. I again.

Dolf. [R.] This is the third time. What's the matter? Havn't you seen the old gentleman yet?

Roth. Yes, but I want to see *you* now.

Dolf. Why, you're looking quite out of sorts. Been taking

some of your own physic? That's bad; ought to have consulted me first. Where's your pulse? [*Tries to get at his wrists.*]

Roth. 'Tisn't that. Drugs won't cure me. It's a very bad case. [*Crosses to* R.]

Dolf. [*Looks at him suspiciously and turns him half round.*] Indeed! who is she?

Roth. You guess it right off. What a splendid doctor you make.

Dolf. I should think so. Now, out with it. Give me the name.

Roth. It's the daughter of old Mr. Bunker.

Dolf. Little Linda. By Jove, Mr. Apothecary, when it comes to taking a dose of matrimony, you mix a very pleasant prescription for yourself. Does she love you?

Roth. I can't find out. I want to get an interview with the old man so as to come to the daughter, but he slips me. He is always on the run, so that a man is dead trying to keep up with him. But I've come to the house again, and this time I come to you, and I say: what do you advise? [*Sits.*]

Dolf. I advise you to consult the young lady. Now that you are here, make a long visit, and if fortune is resolved to favor you, it will bring the lovely maiden within speaking distance. I'll arrange the interview, and in five minutes you complete the fascination.

Roth. [*Rises.*] Five minutes won't do. I should like to have about three-quarters of an hour. I couldn't find the words any sooner. [*Crosses to* L.]

Dolf. The greatest orators have been gravelled on such occasions. Write it down and get it by heart. Sh! here's the mother; make a good impression on *her.*

MRS. BUNKER *enters,* R.

Mrs. Bunker. Pardon me, Doctor, I did not know you had company. [*To Roth.*] Mr. Hoffmeister, I believe? [*Crosses to Dolf.*]

Roth. [*Bowing repeatedly, about to shake hands with Mrs. B., as she crosses to Dolf.*] I have the honor to catch you again.

Dolf. [*To Mrs. B.*] My friend is very busy. [*Crosses to Roth.*] Go to my room and get to work. [*To Mrs. B.*] The poor fellow is preparing a speech.

Roth. [L.] Doctor!

Dolf. [C.] Upon the disturbed cerebral functions of persons in love; he has called on me for assistance in developing the first approaches of the malady. I'm going to help him. [*Crosses to* L.]

Mrs. B. [*To Roth, crosses to* C.] If the Doctor helps you, there's nothing to fear. [*Smiles at Dolf, who is puzzled by her look.*]

Roth. [*Crosses to* C.] See here! don't guy a fellow. [*Goes up.*]

Mrs. B. I won't disturb you a moment, gentlemen; but I'm about to give some orders. One question, Doctor, would you like eels for dinner? [*Giving both hands to Dolf, who crosses to* C.]

Dolf. You are really too good. You're going to spoil me.

Mrs. B. I wish you to retain the pleasantest recollections of our home.

Dolf. I was never happier. Your hospitality is imprinted on my heart. [*Takes her hand.*] I would like eels.

Mrs. B. [*Warmly.*] Fried or stewed? [*Wrings his hands.*]

Dolf. Stewed. [*Wrings her hands.*]

Mrs. B. Sauce piquante?

Dolf. Anyway *you* prepare them. [*To Roth.*] Now then, Galen, we'll get up an oration that will carry your auditor by storm. [*Exeunt,* C. R.]

BUNKER *enters,* L. D., *with hat on, in haste.*

Bunker. Good-bye, my dear.

Mrs. B. You are not going out again?

Bun. Again? Of course; I've got everything to attend to.

Mrs. B. I must have a talk with you, and you're never home a minute.

Bun. [*Irritated, loud.*] Now, what is it?

Mrs. B. Not so loud. That stupid apothecary is in there.

Bun. Has he come again? He sticks to me like one of his own leeches. If we get sick and get into his clutches, he'll not leave us this side of the grave.

Mrs. B. [R.] What does he want with you?

Bun. I don't know. He's got the most infernal long stories about his childhood and the confluence of the Necker. I believe it's a sort of harmless insanity; don't send to his shop for anything, he'll poison us. Now, what do you want?

Mrs. B. [*Sits,* R.] Do sit down a moment.

Bun. [*Sits, testily.*] Heavens! Well, here I am; what is it? [*Drums on table.*]

Mrs. B. Do you know that Linda is eighteen? We must think of her future. She has got to be married some time or other.

Bun. [*Starts up.*] This is a pretty time to talk about that.

Mrs. B. [*Detains him.*] It's the very time to talk about it. [*He sits and drums.*] You never think of the girl.

Bun. There's no hurry, somebody will come along.

Mrs. B. I'd like to know who—leave off drumming on the table—there's not a decent match for her in the place. [*Produces list.*] Here's a list I made out. I had to check them off one by one as each became engaged. Not a soul left. Look at it.

Bun. Why, it's a regular bachelor's directory. [*Drums.*]

Mrs. B. Certainly. Every mother at Narragansett Pier has one by heart, if not in writing. Leave off drumming. So here it is as plain as two and two make four, that she must die an old maid unless some lucky accident— [BUN. *rises.*]

Bun. All right. We'll wait for the accident. It won't probably occur to-day.

Mrs B. [*Detains him, closing on him.*] The accident has arrived!

Bun. What?

Mrs. B. [*Smiling.*] Guess who it is?

Bun. No conundrums, my dear. I'm really busy.

Mrs. B. Well then, it's our guest, Doctor Van Tassel.

Bun. He wants to marry her? Did he tell you?

Mrs. B. Not exactly, but I see what I see, my eyes are sharp. [*Crosses to* L.]

Bun. [*Rises.*] Well, you keep a sharp lookout, and when you see anything more, let me know. [*Going up* L.]

Mrs. B. [*Irritated, rises.*] You don't take the slightest interest in your family.

Bun. My dear, at the proper time, I'll take the deepest interest—don't you be afraid of that. If the young man is profoundly stricken he'll see me and we'll talk about it. [*Going.*]

Mrs. B. [*Following.*] Well, then, you havn't any objection?

Bun. 'If he hasn't, I havn't. [*Runs off,* C. L.]

Mrs. B. [*Returning.*] Thank heaven, that load is off my mind. My poor dear child will be happy.

LINDA *enters,* C. L.

Linda. Mamma, Telka is here. [*Gets* L.]

TELKA *enters,* C. L., *hat in hand.*

Telka. Good morning, Mrs. Bunker. [*Takes her hand and brings her down.*] Is it yes or no?

Mrs. B. [R.] Yes or no to what, child?

Tel. The Colonel is going to have music on the lawn and we want you to come.

Linda. Oh, mamma, do let's go.

Mrs. B. You forget our guest, the doctor. [*Crosses to* c.]

Tel. He'll come, of course. He's got to come. He'll be ordered over. [*To Linda.*] Isn't he a delightful fellow? [*Crosses to* c.]

Linda. [*Indifferent.*] Oh, he'll pass. [*Goes up to piano,* L.]

Tel. [*Mimics.*] "Oh, he'll pass." He has evidently not made an impression.

Mrs. B. [*Aside to Tel.*] Sh! she won't betray herself.

Tel. [*Discreetly.*] I understand.

Mrs. B. [*Same.*] Try to draw her out. [*Finger to lips, mysteriously, aloud.*] I know you two children have a great deal to say to each other. [*Aside to Tel.*] Be cautious.

Tel. [*Same.*] I'll get it out of her in five minutes. [MRS. B. *nods, winks and exits,* R.]

Linda. [*Bringing down Tel. hurriedly.*] Telka, I've something to confide in you.

Tel. Ah! [*Aside.*] She's going to let it out herself.

Linda. Do you remember our discussion about love at first sight?

Tel. [*Breathlessly.*] Yes!

Linda. You were right. There *is* such a thing.

Tel. How did you find it out?

Linda. By experience. Everything happened as you described. Instantaneous fever—electric shocks—a feeling that we had known each other for years.

Tel. Who is he?

Linda. I wouldn't dare to tell you.

Tel. It don't matter, for I've changed my mind. Love at first sight is all stuff. [*Crosses to* L.]

Linda. [*Astonished.*] What?

Tel. I have investigated the subject in the cold light of reason, and have come to the conclusion that the whole thing is imaginary. It's a beautiful dream from which we wake—in the dark.

Linda. But it was you who insisted—

Tel. I was dreaming. Now I know better. There is nothing at first sight [*Tragically seizes her arm,*] but hatred!

Linda. [*Shrinking.*] Telka!

Tel. [*Maintaining her grasp and excited.*] Linda, I must tell you all or my heart will burst. There is some one in our house —I hate *him*. [*Crosses to* R.]

Linda. Not the Colonel?

Tel. [*Laughing bitterly.*] The Colonel? No! A little, paltry, insignificant subordinate—he'll never be a colonel, he hasn't got the heart nor the brains, nor the push. If you only knew [*Crosses to* L.] how that man has behaved to me.

Linda. [*Takes her hand.*] Confide in me.

Tel. I detested him from the first, and of course I showed it plainly; well, he, instead of becoming attentive and trying to overcome my dislike by a profusion of graceful courtesies—what do you think he did? He avoided me.

Linda. Is it possible?

Tel. He cuts me dead and is courting Milly. But if he thinks I care, he's mistaken. I'll punish him. [*Crosses to* R.] I'll make him feel so small that he'll go down on his knees yet to me, and I'll laugh in his face.

Linda. Quite proper. But how will you do it?

Tel. Oh, I don't know; but I'm quite sure nothing is easier. I've begun already. [*Coming to her.*] I had a bouquet placed in his room. When he came out I met him with the most languishing glances. My object is to persuade him that I'm desperately smitten. I had my first triumph this afternoon. He asked me what was my favorite uniform. I said yellow. His is white, you know. Then he inquired which was my favorite regiment. I told him the 99th. His is the 77th, you know. You ought to have seen his expression. He became purple with suppressed feeling.

Linda. Where did you learn such deception?

Tel. At school, of course. [*Crosses to* L.] I got it before I was half through moral philosophy.

Linda. [*Gushingly.*] But Telka, think how dreadful if he should really fall in love and propose.

Tel. [*Triumphantly.*] Oh, if he only would. That's what I'm working for. I'd make him remember that proposal if he lived to be a thousand years old. You don't know how I detest that man. [*Crosses to* R.]

DOLF *enters,* C. R.

Dolf. Excuse me, ladies, I—I—think I left a book somewhere. [*Goes to piano,* L., *and beckons to Linda, unperceived by Tel.* LINDA *goes to him.*] A friend of mine in the apothecary business lent it to me.

Linda. [*Nods, looks back at Tel. quickly.*] Shall I help you look for it? [*Crosses* C. *up to Dolf.*]

Tel. [*Aside.*] They understand each other. "Oh, he'll pass," will he? It's too transparent. [*Watches them, takes stage* R.]

Dolf. [*Aside to Linda.*] There's some one in my room who wants to speak to you on a very important subject; can you guess who it is?

Linda. [*Same.*] The little apothecary.

Dolf. Be kind to him. Give him a hearing.

Linda. [*Crosses to* C.] Thank you. [*Comes to Tel., confused.*] Dear Telka, I have a favor to ask of you, but I don't know exactly how to do it.

Tel. [R.] I'll help you. You want me to go away.

Linda. You won't be angry?

Tel. Certainly not.

Linda. Somebody has something important to tell me.

Tel. [*Glances at Dolf.*] So I should imagine.

Linda. I really don't know what it can be.

Tel. Indeed! [*Loud and pointedly.*] Perhaps the book you are looking for is in your mamma's room. I'll go and see. [*Maliciously.*] Don't be vexed if it takes me some time to find it. I'll be as long as I can. [*Exits,* R. D., *laughing.*]

Dolf. [*Crosses to* R. *and turns back.*] One word. Give him time—plenty of time; he's in a dreadful state. [*Goes to* C. L. *and calls.*] Ahem! [LINDA *goes up* R.]

ROTH *enters, trembling,* C. L.

Dolf. [*Aside to him.*] There she is, all alone; you're perfectly safe, the other young lady has gone to keep mamma out of the way. I'll stand guard at the window and watch the front door. If any one comes, I'll give the signal with my handkerchief.

Roth. My heart's in my diaphragm.

Dolf. Take a pill or something. You must carry a few boluses about you.

Roth. [*Feels his throat.*] Now its creeping up to my pharynx.

Dolf. [*Slapping him on back.*] Swallow it, and speak out boldly. Remember, I'm blind and deaf. [*Crosses to* L.] Watch the handkerchief. [*Goes to window and looks out.*] It's a remarkably fine day.

Roth. [*Timidly clears his throat—pulls at the legs of his pantaloons to straighten them, looks towards Dolf for aid, heaving sigh.*] Hem! hem!

Linda. [*Turns innocently.*] Ahem! ahem! [*Pause.*] Oh, is it you, Mr. Hoffmeister? How you startled me.

Roth. I beg you will pardon the liberty—

Linda. [*Sits.*] Won't you be seated?

Roth. If you permit—[*Aside, as he drops in chair.*] My legs are all gone. [*To Linda.*] I—

Linda. You—

Roth. No, I don't. You—

Linda. I—

Dolf. [*Aside.*] The conversation don't seem to be very lively. [*Clock strikes six.*]

Roth. Wasn't that six ?

Linda. Was it ?

Roth. [*Drawing nearer.*] Do you remember the first time I saw you—when you came into my shop and asked for a glass of soda water—vanilla flavor—with plenty of cream ? Do you recollect what o'clock it was?

Dolf. [*Aside. Leans out at window.*] He's getting along.

Linda. It was somewhere about twelve, wasn't it ?

Roth. [*Leaning over nearer.*] It was a quarter past eleven of the happiest day of my life. [*Their heads touch, and they start back.*]

Linda. How accurate you are.

Roth. I went home, and at twenty minutes past twelve I finished a poem. [*Puts on spectacles—takes paper from pocket.*] Here—no, that's a recipe for the mumps. Here—no, that's my washing bill from the Chinese laundry. Ah, here it is. [*Reads.*]

> Once upon a midnight windy,
> I dreamed a dream of little Lindy,
> I thought as gazing from my winder
> Across the street I saw dear Linder—
> My heart was burnt into a cinder,
> As—as—Oh, Miss Linder.

Linda. Do you write many poems ?

Roth. No, not as a general thing, but I felt so sick—I mean —so bad—when I put my hand in my pocket, I found one of your gloves, that I must have brought away without knowing. I laid it on the table before me, and then I commenced to think of the other.

Linda. Of the other glove ?

Roth. Yes—and the thought came into my mind, that two and two makes a pair—no, I mean that one and one makes a pair.

Linda. I have the other one.

Roth. Yes, and I have the tother one. [*Aside, wiping his forehead.*] Now I don't know how to go any further ! [DOLF *shakes handkerchief violently behind his back.*]

Roth. [*Sees the signal and jumps up.*] Good heavens !

Linda. [*Rising—alarmed.*] What is the matter ?

Roth. He gives the sign. Some one is coming, and I havn't told you.

Linda. [R.] Told me what ?

Roth. [*With a burst.*] That I love you.

Linda. [*Averts her face.*] Oh ! [*Stage*, R.]

Roth [*Following her.*] Oh, please don't be angry. I wouldn't make you angry for anything. Only he's shaking his handkerchief all the time. That is—yes, I want you to know I love you, even if I died the next minute. Do speak to me. [*Takes her hand—sings.*] "Oh, speak to me." [*Kneels.*]

Linda. [*Head averted.*] I can't speak.

Roth. [*Draws her to him.*] And I can't speak. [*Suddenly springs up and hugs her.* DOLF *suddenly turns.*]

Dolf. [*Closes window, advances to Roth, swings him round, as he does so,* ROTH *catches the end of a long bow that Linda wears round her neck, and drags it off—turns round upon Dolf, embraces him, and is lifted on to the table, his feet on chair. He kisses the ribbon frantically.*] I might shake forever. Good heavens! Behave yourselves! Here's one of the fellows coming. He's just at the door.

Linda. What a pity, just at this moment. [*Runs off,* R. D.]

Roth. [*Calls after her.*] I'll speak to your father and mother, this very day.

Dolf. [*Restraining him*] Stop! That'll do. .

Roth. [*Clasps him in his arms.*] I must hug something or somebody.

SYDAM *enters,* C.

Sydam. I'm afraid I'm spoiling a tender scene.

Dolf. [C.] Not at all. [*Introducing.*] An old chum at the medical college, and now established as head apothecary of this flourishing village.

Syd. Charmed! Doctor and druggist? We only want the undertaker. [*Fixes himself at mirror, takes out brushes to do his back hair.*]

Roth. [*To Dolf, going up* C.] Now I'll go home, put on my claw-hammer coat, come back, and speak to her father.

Dolf. All right, Galen.

Roth. Good-bye. [*Hugs him, shakes his hands, then runs to* SYD., *stops, dodges around him, grasps his hands with the brushes, shakes them and runs out, leaving* SYD. *astonished. As* ROTH *goes off,* SCIPIO *enters,* ROTH *hugs him and runs off,* C. L.]

Syd. [*Turns to Dolf.*] Got anybody with you?

Dolf. No.

Syd. Before Dexter drops in on us, I want to talk to you [*Brushing hair.*] It's in the strictest confidence, all among the boys, you know. I say—you know—I've been acting in the silliest kind of manner—I've fallen in love, you know.

Dolf. Nonsense.

Syd. [*Serious.*] It *is* nonsense, but what's to be done?

Dolf. [*Shrugs his shoulders.*] I really can't say.

Syd. You must look seriously at the matter, because it's no joke.

Dolf. [R.] Indeed! [*Aside.*] The second serious case to-day. [*Crosses to* C.]

Syd. The young person lives in the house where the colonel stops.

Dolf. [*Alarmed.*] Hey? What's that?

Syd. She's a young Russian.

Dolf. [*Relieved.*] Oh, Telka—I know her. [*Crosses to* L.]

Syd. [*Seated in rocking-chair.*] Then, of course, you understand I couldn't help it.

Dolf. [L.] Of course not.

Syd. When my condition became clear to my own mind, I began to proceed in a straightforward manner. You know the companion—Miss Milly, or Millicent, I think.

Dolf. I believe I do.

Syd. Nice sort of girl. To get in her confidence I paid her particular attention. You know how well I do that sort of thing; but she didn't respond—seems to be somewhat limited. [*Taps forehead.*]

Dolf. Poor thing.

Syd. I managed to learn, however, that my charmer hasn't a dollar. But that's immaterial; *I* haven't a dollar; but my governor's always at me to settle down, and when I settle on a young lady, of course he'll settle on me—that is, if she'll agree to settle, too.

Dolf. Then it's plain sailing.

Syd. Not exactly; for I've got to propose twice—first to her, and then to her papa.

Dolf. All quite regular, I don't see what I can do. [*Crosses to* R.] You don't want me to ask the young lady, do you?

Syd. No, as soon as I'm alone with her, I can manage that; but there's the other—her father, you know. It seems the old gentleman, for some unaccountable reason, is a Russian, and lives in Russia, in a gold mine or coal mine, or somewhere. Nobody knows his designs with respect to his daughter; he may object to a foreigner.

Dolf. Then why not communicate with him before you propose?

Syd. It takes such a deuce of a time—just think—Russia!

Dolf. Why not cable?

Syd. Cable?

Dolf. Something in this style: "An American gentleman of good family, respectfully asks your permission to propose for the hand of your daughter." Signed "Thorpe Sydam, Captain, etc."

There you are, straightforward and sensible. That will please him.

Syd. I'll do it. [*Rises.*] Couldn't we add, "of pleasing appearance." Only three words more, it won't cost much?

Dolf. If you think it necessary.

Syd. I suppose, though, he'd infer that.

Dolf. I don't think it would have any weight. Would you like to write the dispatch now?

Syd. [L.]' Can I use your room?

Dolf. Certainly.

PAUL DEXTER *enters*, C. L.

Paul. Morning, doctor. [*To Syd.*] Are you off?

Syd. Only to send a telegram. [*Going*, C.] *Apropos*, doctor, don't say anything about it. Though you needn't mind Dexter, he knows my secrets, all the same among the boys, and he's one of us. [*Exits*, C. R.]

Dolf. [*Motions with head towards Syd.'s exit.*] He's is love again.

Paul. [*Sits*, L.] I know it. Curious. But he's a good fellow, spite of these little weaknesses; I wish him joy with his pretty Russian.

Dolf. Don't you like her?

Paul. Oh, yes. Charming creature, she excites my sincerest pity. [*Crosses to* R.]

Dolf. [*Aside, watching him.*] Does she? This is patient No. 3, or I'm much mistaken.

Paul. She's an April beauty—sunshine, hailstorms, blue sky and thunder.

Dolf. Girlish humors.

Paul. Save me from such humors. I tell you, Van Tassel, she's either an overgrown child or a practiced coquette.

Dolf. Oh, you're on a war footing with her.

Paul. No open declaration yet; preliminary strategy only. She's manœuvering to take me captive and chain me to her triumphal car. She never made a worse mistake. If she wants to play with me, she has selected the wrong man; I can be very obstinate at times.

SYDAM *enters*, C. R.

Sydam. I took the liberty of sending your boy to the telegraph office. By the way—I hope the old gentleman will find somebody to translate the message. Ah! here come the ladies.

TELKA *and* LINDA *enter*, R. D., *the young men bow—general greeting.* TELKA *has a roll of music.*

Telka. [*Aside to Linda.*] Now, Linda, remember what ·I just told you. You'll see that these young military persons are all only too anxious to play the cavalier to a lady to need any incentive of reward.

Syd. [*Advances to them.*] Well, ladies, can I serve you. Consider me at your orders. Command me.

Tel. [*Looks at Paul, then turns away.*] The others are silent. Did you notice those lovely flowers, Linda, growing on the island opposite. I'd give anything for a bunch of them for the ball to-night. I have it. I offer a prize, my first waltz to-night, to the gentleman who will row across and get me some of those wild roses. [*To Paul.*] Is the reward not sufficient, Mr. Dexter? [*Crosses to him.*]

Paul. [*Polite, but cold.*] It is too great, Miss Telka, I am quite ready to get you the roses, but I must renounce the prize. I don't dance.

Tel. [*Suppressed anger.*] You do not dance?

Paul. Not this evening. [*Up* C., *talks to Dolf.*]

Syd. But I dance, I'm found of dancing—and I don't dance half badly, I'll bring the roses. [*Goes up.*]

Linda. Can you row?

Syd. Like a boatman.

Linda. But if—can you swim?

Syd. Like a fish. [*Exits,* C. L.]

Dolf. [*Aside to Paul.*] He can't do either. He'll be drowned.

Tel. [*Who has been looking at Paul, aside to Linda.*] Did you hear that man?

Linda. It was not very gallant.

Tel. [*Crosses to piano.*] Outrageous! But wait.

MRS. BUNKER *enters*, R. D. DOLF *goes to meet her and comes down.*

Mrs. Bunker. Doctor! [*Aside.*] I'll encourage him to speak. Linda has told me nothing—but a mother's eyes are sharp.

Dolf. What, you know?

Mrs. B. I believe I know everything.

Dolf. And you give your consent?

Mrs. B. With all my heart, I am sure my daughter will be happy.

4

Dolf. I can promise that.

Mrs. B. I don't know why I took such a fancy to you from the first. I could fold you to my heart like a son.

· *Dolf.* [*Astonished.*] My dear madam. [*Crosses to* R., LINDA *comes down* R.]

Mrs. B. Not before these people, of course. By and by. [*Goes up.*]

Dolf. What a demonstrative parent. If she folds me to her heart for helping on the match, what'll she do to Hoffmeister? [*Goes to Linda,* R.]

Tel. [*At piano,* L., *leaning on forward end. To Paul.*] I saw your horses to-day—the black is a splendid animal. [MRS. B. *observes Dolf and Linda.*]

Paul. Very kind, I'm sure.

Tel. Do you know I've the greatest desire to try him.

Paul. He's at your service, but permit me to warn you—

Tel. [*Resolutely.*] I know how to handle the reins; there's nothing I can't manage.

Paul. Perhaps. But you don't know this animal. [*Crosses to* C.] He needs a steady grip. Whimsical management—changing from candy to lashes—will make him vicious; he might throw you.

Tel. That would be exceedingly impolite.

Paul. But it would show the mettle of the beast. [*Turns to Linda and converses with her.*]

Tel. [*Looks after him indignantly.*] He leaves me again and goes to her; this is really too much, I could cry with vexation. [*Rises and goes to window.*]

Mrs. B. [*Observing Paul. Aside.*] I wish he wouldn't intrude on the dear children's happiness.

Tel. [*Dries her tears resolutely.*] No, I will not cry; I'll have an understanding at any price. [*To Paul, with forced politeness.*] Mr. Dexter.

Paul. [*Politely.*] At your service. [*Bows to Linda and goes to Tel.*]

Tel. Mr. Dexter, let us be open and honest. You are angry with me.

Paul. I?

Tel. Don't deny it. This morning you wanted to accompany my song, I refused. You were offended, but I could not help it. I was nervous and had a headache.

Paul. No apology is required.

Tel. Well, I have the song here; will you accompany me, now?

Paul. [*Politely.*] Pardon *me. I* have a headache, *now.* [TEL. *crushes the music in her hands.*]

Linda. [*Goes to Tel.*] Be calm.

Tel. [*Furious.*] I am ready now for anything desperate.

BUNKER *enters, hurriedly,* C.

Bunker. A nice mess. See here, all you; here's one of the officers has fallen overboard. [*All excitement.*]

All. [*Startled.*] An officer—who—who—who is it?

Bun. He was rowing across the river.

Tel. [*Starts.*] Mr. Sydam?

Mrs. B. Is he drowned?

Bun. Not exactly, but he's so wet that he won't be dry in a week.

Dolf. [*Crosses to him.*] Where is he?

Bun. In my room. I sent him some of my own clothes, they were dryer than his.

Dolf. I'll go to him at once. } *Together. Exeunt hur-*

Paul I'll send him my servant. } *riedly,* C. L.

Mrs. B. How did it happen?

Bun. No matter about that, now. Go and make some tea, boiling hot.

Linda. [*Running off,* R. D.] I'll do it.

Tel. I'll go with you. [*Exeunt,* R. D.]

Mrs. B. What a shocking accident! [*Exits,* R. D.]

Bun. I hope my clothes will fit him.

Runs up hastily and almost upsets ROTH, *who enters,* C. L., *in full dress, white kids, etc.*

Roth. [L.] Mr. Bunker, I have the honor to wish you good morning.

Bun. [R.] Heavens! Here's that apothecary again.

Roth. [*Solemnly.*] Honored sir, and arbiter of my destinies, I come to you with a swelling heart. What I am about to say—

Bun. [R.] There's no getting rid of him.

Roth. What I am about to say will scarcely surprise you, when you glance at my festive attire. From my earliest childhood—

Bun. [*Turning away.*] I really have no time, at present.

Roth. But you *must* listen to me. From my earliest childhood—

Bun. [*Going, aside.*] He'll never get out of the cradle. Very sorry. [*Aside.*] Confound his impudence. [*Exits,* C. L.]

Roth. It is strange. This man never has time. But here is the mother.

Mrs. Bunker *enters,* R. D, *with tea-kettle, and is crossing, when* Roth *waylays her.*

Roth. Honored lady! Animated by—

Mrs. Bunker. Oh, it's you.

Roth. I bring you a swelling heart.

Mrs. B. Which is best to give a drowned man, spirits or chamomile tea?

Roth. A drowned man? Chamomile tea?

Mrs. B. Thanks. I thought so. [*Exits, quickly,* C. L.]

Roth. I guess I've come at another bad time.

Dolf *enters, and speaks back,* C. R.

Dolf. I'll attend to it.

Roth. [R.] Thank goodness you arrive. What is the matter with the parents?

Dolf. Here, make yourself useful—run and tell them to get out a wagon. [*Hurries Roth up.*]

Roth. Yes, but I'd like to know.

Dolf. No time—no time—run as quick as your legs can carry you. [*Goes back to door.*]

Roth. Nobody has no time—I can never get a word in. [*Exits,* C. L.]

Dolf. [*At door.*] Come in, old boy, no one here. [*Comes down,* L.]

Sydam. [*Putting in head,* C. R.] Are you sure? I wouldn't like to show off in this costume.

Dolf. [L. C.] Of course not. Come in.

Sydam *enters,* C. L.—*wears trowsers too large and too short. Coat too large and too long. Vest too loose and too long. Hair straight and wet; wearing very large slippers and an eye-glass. Looks down at himself.*

Sydam. Awful, isn't it.

Dolf. [L.] Not too awful, just awful enough.

Syd. It's all the same among the boys, but I wouldn't like any one else to see me in this rig.

Dolf. Why not? Just the least bit of a misfit. [*Crosses to* L.]

Syd. [*At mirror.*] I generally look as well in civilian dress as in uniform, but it seems to me that the man must have an extraordinary figure; his clothes are too short, too long, too tight and too loose all at once.

Dolf. How did you fall overboard?

Syd. [*Steps to mantel and examines bottles, gets perfume and sprinkles on his clothes—advances.*] The confounded thing was going very well, and I was pulling like the deuce, when I grounded on a mud-bank. I got up to shove her off—leaned too heavily on the oar—it stuck in the mud—the boat shot out ten feet and left me in the water.

Dolf. It wasn't very deep, then?

Syd. The mud was, and I was wrong end up in it.

Dolf. But you feel generally well now?

Syd. [*Hand to waist.*] There's a sense of fulness here.

Dolf. Swallowed a lot of water? Not used to it. I'll fetch you some peppermint.

Syd. Anything. Nothing can taste worse.

Dolf. They'll have a wagon here, directly, to take you home. [*Goes out, c. r.*]

Syd. [*Takes flowers out of his pocket.*] I got her the roses. Saved them from the wreck. They are slightly demoralized, but they'll soon recover. I'll deposit them here. [*Goes to table, and puts them in vase.*]

TELKA *enters, r. d., with small tray and cup of tea—does not perceive him.*

Telka. Here is the tea. Here it is.

Syd. Good gracious! [*Jumps behind screen.*]

Tel. Here's your tea. [*Puts tea on table, turns to look for him, and sees his head above screen.*] Mr. Sydam, what are you doing there?

Syd. [*Glass in eye, edging away to c. and l. c.*] Nothing.

Tel. Then come out and drink your tea.

Syd. [c.] It's quite pleasant here.

Tel. You're playing hide and seek with me.

Syd. No, but I beg to be allowed to bloom in retirement, like the violet. The fact is, I've got on the good old gentleman's fatigue dress, and look slightly ridiculous.

Tel. A man of sense ought to be above such trifling considerations.

Syd. Of course, especially before a woman of sense. But I can't rise to the occasion.

Tel. Don't you want the tea.

Syd. I'm going to have some peppermint in a minute.

Tel. [r.] I will make you a proposition. I'll sit here [*Sits in rocker*], and turn my back—there. Now be sensible, and drink your tea.

Syd. [*Comes down to table, holds the back of her chair, to prevent her turning round.*] Very good, but you mustn't look.

Tel. I shall never forgive myself; it was my childish whim that caused your mishap.

Syd. I am only too happy at having won the prize which you set upon these flowers; may I lay them at your feet? [*Stands behind her chair, and hands roses over her shoulder. She is about to turn.*] Don't look! [*Holds her chair firmly.*]

Tel. [*Looking at roses.*] This is really touching.

Syd. [*Aside.*] She seems to be touched. [*Fixes his hair.*] Perhaps this is the time to speak. [*Aloud.*] Do you know that your goodness encourages me to make a confession?

Tel. Indeed! How interesting! Have you drunk your tea?

Syd. No, but I will. [*Takes cup up.*] It often happens that in moments of danger, all that was confused and uncertain in one's mind, becomes suddenly clear and distinct, like—like a dark landscape lit by a flash of lightning. That is what happened to me when I felt myself going over.

Tel. What struck you at that moment?

Syd. [*The cup is hot, and he changes it from hand to hand. Draws out large cotton handkerchief.*] I felt— [*Stuffs handkerchief back hastily.*] I felt—I felt—my whole life growing to one point—all my thoughts centering in one idea—all my senses wrought to one perception—this was that I loved—that I loved passionately—madly—a being I saw before me, as I see her now—

Tel. [*Turns unconsciously.*] You loved me? [*She no sooner sees him than she begins to laugh, and in spite of all her exertions, bursts into uncontrollable mirth.*]

Syd. [*Dropping cup and saucer, and dodging behind screen.*] I knew it! The moment she saw me I was lost.

MR. *and* MRS. BUNKER *and* LINDA *appear,* C., *and laugh at the tableau; between the two fires,* SYDAM *dodges, placing his screen so as to hide himself from either.*

QUICK CURTAIN

ACT IV.

SCENE. — *Justice Winthrop's grounds. A summer-house at* R., *with large window, and bench under it, also a door with steps leading to same. Shrubbery and bench* C., *statue of Cupid with bow and arrow behind bench. View of park at back. Color-guard and maid servants looking on at back. Dance: Military Schottische introduced. After the dance all exeunt.*

SOLOMON *enters from summer-house,* R., SOPHIE *enters with tray of refreshments from* L. 2 E.

Solomon. Here you come at last. You're wanted everywhere.

Sophie. Well, I can't be everywhere at once.

Sol. You'd be a little more useful if you didn't stop every minute to gape at the soldiers.

Sophie. I'm sure when people pay one the compliment of looking at one, one may look back. [*Exits,* R. U. E.]

Sol. [*Closes summer-house door.*] There ain't a woman in the place but what's gone crazy since that regiment's come to town.

WINTHROP *enters,* L. U. E.

Winthrop. What are you doing there, Solomon?

Sol. [*Points to summer-house.*] I have just put the fireworks in the summer-house, sir. I thought they'd be safer there. Where are we going to set off the balloons, sir?

Win. Fireworks? Balloons? Do you want to burn my house down?

Sol. Mrs. Winthrop ordered them, sir.

Win. [*Mollified.*] Oh! Well, I'll consult with her about it. If she forgets them, don't you remind her·

Sol. Shall we hang any lanterns here, sir?

Win. No; nobody comes here after dark. Keep them all near the house.

Sol. All right, sir. [*Exits,* L. U. E.]

Mrs. Winthrop. [*Outside, calling in distance.*] Dar-ling! where are you?

Win. [*Answering.*] Here I am! with Cupid.

MRS. WINTHROP *enters,* R. 2 E.

Mrs. Winthrop. I've been looking for you everywhere. Oh,

there you are!   Have you thought about the band?   They must have some refreshments, and there actually seems to be a thousand of them.

Win.   [L.]   I've attended to that.   The sandwiches have come up in two wagons.

Mrs. W.   [R.]   It was really very kind of the Colonel to have the regimental band play for us.

Win.   Very.   They've attracted the whole population.   Nothing is wanted but a sign up, "Ball and concert this evening; admission free," and we'll have standing room only.

· *Mrs. W.*   But I only invited our most intimate friends.

Win.   The town has invited itself.   Where is Telka?

Mrs. W.   Somewhere in the garden, I suppose.

Win.   And Milly?

Mrs. W.   [*Testily*]   I don't know.   [*Crosses to* R.]

Win.   [*Sighs.*]   I may as well be satisfied.

Mrs. W.   You're a perfect fidget about those girls.

Win.   Because I never get a sight of them any more.   It was by mere accident that I saw Telka this afternoon as she came galloping up with the lieutenant.

Mrs. W.   But the Colonel was galloping with them.

Win.   I know it, they nearly ran over me.

COLONEL *enters,* R. U. E., *with* TELKA *on his arm, in lively conversation.*

Colonel.   My dear Mr. Winthrop, the ladies have been kind enough to show me over the park; you have a beautiful place. Everything to make a man happy.

Win.   [R. C.]   Yes, nothing is wanting.   I was just remarking to my wife—

Mrs. W.   [*Interrupting him.*]   The music and uniforms make a lovely picture.

Win.   Yes, it quite gives you the idea of a camp.

PAUL *enters,* L. 2 E., *on duty.*

Col.   [*Crosses to Paul.*]   Wherever the soldiers are they make things lively.   [*To Paul.*]   Have you anything for me, Dexter?

Paul.   Report, sir.   [*Gives paper.*]

Col.   [*Glances at it, brings Paul down.*]   Very well.   Is the bivouac attended to?

Paul.   Yes, sir.

Col.   I'll inform you when we make the rounds.

Paul.   Any further orders, Colonel?

Col. [*Aside to him.*] Yes, I have a rather delicate mission for you, my dear Dexter. I notice that our host evinces a particular concern about his niece, the young Russian lady.

Paul. I've noticed it, too.

Col. I wish the young officers would not pay her too marked attention. If you could use some tact in the matter—you understand—hint to them my desire—do it without letting the young lady know.

Paul. I'll do my best, Colonel.

Col. It would oblige me greatly. [PAUL *salutes and goes off,* L. 2 E.]

Telka. [*Coming down, sits* R.] This is my favorite spot, Colonel, of which I told you. There is the summer-house, where I waste paper and pencil in my leisure hours.

Col. Very charming, but, for a young lady, quite as dangerous as romantic.

Enter BUNKER *and* MRS. BUNKER, LINDA *and* DOLF. *They greet Win. and Mrs. W.,* L. 2 E.

Tel. Dangerous? Why?

Col. [*Points to statue.*] Are you not afraid of Cupid? There he stands, arrow in hand.

Tel. [*Saunters round to* L. H.] But he never hits the mark.

Col. He might—by accident. [*The groups mingle.* COL. *gives Mrs. W. his arm, exeunt,* R. U. E.]

Dolf. [*Coming down with Linda.*] Trust to me. I'll manage to get him a chance to speak to you.

Linda. [R.] But he's not invited.

Dolf. No matter; he'll slip in with the crowd, and I'll arrange the rest.

Linda. You are so kind; if I could only do you a favor.

Dolf. Would you? Then tell Miss Milly that I shall be walking presently under the trees near the pond.

Linda. I understand.

Dolf. Hush! Discretion! [*They go up.*]

Mrs. Bunker. [*Observing Dolf and Linda.*] Look at them!

Bunker. Who? where? what is it?

Mrs. B. The Doctor and Linda—how happy they seem. Has he spoken to you? [DOLF *exits.*]

Bun. Not yet.

Mrs. B. I don't understand it. And ·he's going away tomorrow; perhaps he's too timid. How can I ask him, if he would like to marry my daughter?

Bun. Have you no regard for her?

Mrs. B.   Yes, and for that reason I can't throw her at his head.   [*They go up.* TEL. *comes down with* LINDA; *they have been talking together.*]

Linda.   [*Frightened.*]   But Telka!

Tel.   Don't speak to me.   I know it's not right.   [*Crosses to* L.]

Linda.   You have actually written to him yourself?

Tel.   Anonymously and in a disguised hand.

Linda.   A rendezvous?   [*Looks round frightened.*]   Do you think he'll come?

Tel.   I hope so.

Linda.   I trust it will end well, but I fear you will repent it.

Tel.   [*With energy, follows her.*]   Have no fear; my only purpose is to punish him.

SYDAM *enters,* L. U. E., *greets Bun. and Mrs. B., and comes down with them.*

Mrs. B.   So you caught cold after all.

Sydam.   [*A little croupy and feeling his throat.*]   Only a little hoarse.

Tel.   I am honestly sorry, Mr. Sydam.

Syd.   [*Crosses to Tel.*]   The Doctor ordered me to go home after that last dance, but I had to offer my excuses personally about that waltz.

Tel.   [*Advances to him.*]   So you will not stay any longer?

Syd.   No.   I have no heart for dancing or music now.   [*Observes Bunker occasionally through his glass, then shakes his head and aside.*]   Strange!   That man wears the oddest clothes I ever saw.

Tel.   [L.]   It seems to me that you are becoming very sentimental.

Syd.   Yes, I noticed it too.   [*Observes Bun.*]

Tel.   [*To Linda.*]   This is the second rebuff to-day.   They are all in a conspiracy to treat me as if I were a child.   [*Goes up with Linda, is joined by Bun. and exeunt,* R. 3 E.]

Syd.   [*To himself,* R.]   Commenced my epitaph after dinner. It'll read well: "Cut off in the flower of his youth as he was cutting a flower for beauty."

Bun.   [*Having noticed Syd.'s looks, inspects himself, going up turns to speak to Syd.*]   Is there anything wrong, Mr. Sydam? You seem to look at me very earnestly.

Syd.   I was wondering why your clothes fitted me so abominably.   *You* don't look so ridiculous in them.

Bun.   [*Swelling out, complaisantly.*]   That's because my figure is better than yours.   [*Exits,* L. U. E.]

Syd. He thinks that a good joke. I can't enjoy it. I'm not in the humor. [*Stage* L.]

DOLF *enters*, R. U. E.

Dolf. What, you here? Go home, take a hot milk punch and we'll have your bronchial tubes all right in the morning.

Syd. [L.] Tubes are all right—the trouble is here. [*Hand on heart.*] I'm doomed. [*Drops into seat*, C.]

Dolf. Have you got the mitten?

Syd. [L. C.] It amounts to the same thing. She doesn't love me. Those infernal clothes did it.

Dolf. [L.] Can't you stand a little laugh?

Syd. From the boys; yes it's all right among the boys. But when the girl you're in love with goes into hysterics at your personal appearance, you are—in short—done for. I've given her up.

Dolf. Very sensible.

Syd. But that's not the end of it. You recollect, I cabled to the old man; now suppose he wires us back his blessing? That would make me more ridiculous than ever, you know? I should be in for it and she'd be out of it.

Dolf. When the answer comes we'll find a way to get out of it too; meanwhile let no one suspect, and act the amiable in your usual delightful manner.

Syd. Delightful? With a voice like a frog's. [*Exits*, L. 2 E.]

SCIPIO *enters with military cloak and fatigue cap*, L. U. E.

Scipio. Report myself, doctor, everything attended to.

Dolf. Very good, wait here. [*Goes up and beckons off*, L.] Come along, no one is here. Pluck up spirit, take heart.

ROTH *enters*, L. U. E., *in evening dress, as in last act.*

Roth. Think what my position is. Not invited! If they see me, they'll show me over the fence, quick.

Dolf. I've provided for that. [*To Scipio.*] Give me the things.

Roth. What have you got?

Dolf. Take off your helmet. [*Points to Roth's high hat.*] And put these on. [*Taking cloak and helmet from Scipio.*] No one will know you in the dark.

Roth. Then Miss Linda, she won't know me—then I came for nothing. [*To Scipio.*] You take care of that hat.

Scipio. All right, sir. [*Exits,* L. U. E.]

Dolf. I intend to lead you by a lonely path, round the house and into the conservatory. There you will sit down patiently until I can give her the information. It may be several hours, but you won't mind that.

Roth. Give her the information right away, so she can sit down several hours with me. You don't know all I've got to tell that girl.

SOPHIE *enters with tray.* ROTH *shrinks close to Dolf.*

Sophie. Will you help yourself, sir?

Dolf. [*Aside to Roth.*] Straighten up or you'll be discovered. Assume a military air. Take some ice cream.

Roth. No, no. I'm all cold now, inside.

Dolf. The girl's looking at you. Be a soldier. Help yourself to a glass of wine. Avert suspicion.

Roth. [*Eagerly.*] Wine! [*Turns to tray and swallows two glassfuls rapidly.*]

Dolf. That's very good, but don't take too much.

Roth. That makes me feel better. Now I can do it. [*Cocks hat on side, winks at Sophie, takes another glass, chucks her under the chin and is violently carried off by* DOLF, L. 2 E.]

Sophie. He's a real soldier. I bet he's been in the regular army. You can tell it by his air? Just like the cook's young man used to act.

Mary Anne. [*Outside,* R. U. E.] Sophie!

Sophie. What is it?

MARY ANNE *enters.*

Mary Anne. I want you, we're going to get up a dance.

Sophie. Where?

Mary. Behind the laundry. We can hear the music, and I'll get plenty of company. [*Looks at tray.*] You've got lots of things left, bring them along.

Sophie. Oh, good gracious! [*Looks round.*] They'll miss me.

Mary. [*Carrying off tray.*] And they'll miss this, too. [*Exits,* R. U. E.]

Sophie. [*Looks off,* L.] Here's somebody coming. [*Exits,* R. U. E.]

PAUL *enters*, L. 2 E., *with note, looks round, sees Cupid.*

Paul. This is the spot, sure enough. [*Reads.*] "Cupid armed, stands in the garden. Be on the spot at which he aims with his arrow. Postscript. 8 P.M." [*Puts up letter.*] The arrow points this way, and it's 8 o'clock. [*Goes up to Cupid and salutes.*] I beg to report myself—present. [*Throws himself on bench.*] Who can it be? If my presentment prove true— [*Suddenly leans forward and looks off.*] Some one coming. It is Telka. [*Gets up and walks unconcernedly about, whistling.*]

TELKA *enters*, R. U. E.

Telka. Mr. Dexter! [*Feigns surprise.*]
Paul. [*Salutes.*] Ah! Miss Telka!
Tel. What brings you to this deserted spot?
Paul. [*Lightly.*] I am in quest of an adventure.
Tel. Indeed, how romantic.
Paul. Isn't it. If you promise not to betray me, I'll confide a secret to your keeping. I have a rendezvous on this very spot.
Tel. With a lady?
Paul. I hope so.
Tel. [*Going.*] In that case I will not intrude.
Paul. Oh, I beg you won't suppose I take the thing seriously. It's a hoax, of course.
Tel. What makes you think that?
Paul. Because I'm not acquainted with any lady who takes sufficient interest in me to write such a billet-doux. [*Produces it.*] Perfumed with violet. I'll keep the blank page for my card case. [*Tears letter in two.*]
Tel. [*Aside.*] How the barbarian treats my billet. [*Aloud.*] So you think it is only a joke?
Paul. I am certain of it. [*Looks at watch.*] It's after 8, and no lady. Unless, of course, it happened to be you. [*Affects laugh.*]
Tel. [*Forcing laugh.*] I? Certainly not. How can you imagine I could ever come to do such a thing? [*Aside, furious.*] He's looking right at me with his mean, sharp, big black, splendid eyes; I'd like to box his ears. [*Crosses to him,* L.]
Paul. [*Laughs.*] Of course, I was only joking. [*Aside.*] It *is* she. [*Aloud.*] I can't be mistaken in the locality, the directions are precise. Read it yourself. [*Hands her the blank leaf.*]
Tel. [*Takes paper passively and does not look at it—aside.*] I would give anything if I had not written it.

Paul. I am right, am I not? There is Cupid.

Tel. [*Crosses to* R.] Yes, and this is the direction of the arrow, so it must be here.

Paul. Indeed! What do you know about the direction of the arrow?

Tel. [*Looking at him surprised.*] Because this letter says so. [*Holding out paper.*]

Paul. Excuse me, it does not say anything. I gave you the blank leaf.

Tel. [*Aside, crumples the letter and throws it down.*] Oh! good heavens!

Paul. So you have seen the letter before?

Tel. [*Controls herself.*] Well, then, since I have betrayed myself so awkwardly, nothing remains but to confess frankly—

Paul. [*Calmly.*] Ah!

Tel. It was written by—a friend of mine.

Paul. A friend of yours?

Tel. I can't tell you the name, of course.

Paul. Of course not. Besides, I don't wish to know it; but if you really love your friend, warn her never again to play so dangerous a game. No matter how innocent her motives might be, she risks entailing on herself life-long misery.

Tel. [*Half aside.*] Never again.

Paul. This time the danger is fortunately averted. Pray return the note to her, with my word of honor to forget the affair from this moment and forever.

Tel. [*Softly.*] I thank you.

Paul. And thus I shall carry but one remembrance with me when I leave this house; the remembrance unclouded but lasting of you. Good-bye. [*Going.*]

Tel. [*After a short struggle.*] I will not tell him a falsehood. [*Calling.*] Mr. Dexter!

Paul. Miss Telka!

Tel. I will tell you the truth. You guessed it from the first —although you were too generous to humiliate me. It was I who wrote the letter in a moment of folly.

Paul. But pray—

Tel. [*Coming down.*] Oh, I know it was not right, but I do not regret, for it gave me the opportunity of knowing one man possessed of an honorable and generous heart. [*Gives hand.*]

Paul. [*Kisses it.*] And you have won a true friend.

Winthrop. [*Outside, calls.*] Telka, where are you?

Tel. [*Alarmed.*] My uncle! [*Crosses to* L.]

Paul. Your uncle, I presume I had better not be seen here.

Tel. No, no, not for the world.

Paul. Have no fear. [*Runs up steps into summer-house.* TEL. *sits on sofa under window.*]

COLONEL *enters with* WINTHROP, R. U. E.

Colonel. [C.] There, I see the folds of a dress among the shrubbery.

Winthrop. [L., *calls.*] Telka!

Tel. Yes, uncle.

Win. [*Crosses to* C.] What are you doing there?

Tel. I? Nothing. You know this is my favorite retreat.

Win. [*Looking round.*] But at this hour and alone! [*Crosses to* C.]

Tel. Yes—quite alone.

Col. [L.] It seems to me then you don't enjoy the company.

Tel. [*Sees Win. going to the summer-house.*] Where are you going, uncle?

Win. [*At foot of steps.*] The fireworks are in here.

Tel. [*Runs up steps and puts her back to door.*] You cannot go in here. [*Locks door and puts key in her pocket.*]

Win. And why not, pray?

Tel. Because—because I've got a surprise for your birthday, and you mustn't see what it is.

Win. Well, I promise not to look round.

Tel. No, no, I've locked the door.

Win. Then you *must* unlock it.

Col. [L.] Don't spoil her little pleasure.

Enter MRS. BUNKER, R. U. E.

Tel. Thanks, Colonel! You stand by me. [*Crosses to Col.*]

Mrs. Bunker. [*Goes to Win.*] Mr. Winthrop, can you tell me where Linda is? I've been looking for her everywhere. [*Rest of scene must be acted rapidly.*]

Win. Linda? I saw her just now in the conservatory with an officer.

Mrs. B. [*Satisfied.*] With an officer? Oh, that's the doctor. [*To Col.*] One of your staff?

Col. [*Crosses to her.*] No, I can quiet your fears on that point, the doctor is promenading with another lady near the pond.

Mrs. B. [C., *alarmed.*] With another lady? [*To Win.*] Then whom did you see with Linda?

Win. I don't know him.

Mrs. B. [*Anxious and goes up.*] I'll find out this very minute.

Tel. I'll go with you. [*They exeunt quickly,* L. U. E.]
Col. I can't understand what has become of Dexter. I told Sydam to send him to me.

MRS. WINTHROP *enters,* R. U. E.

Mrs. Winthrop. Would you believe it—I beg your pardon, Colonel. [*To Win.*] The cook and chambermaid have disappeared.
Win. Gone after some more lieutenants.
Mrs. W. You must find them instantly.
Win. I'd like to know how I'm to do that?

SOLOMON *enters,* R. U. E., *down* C. *to Mrs. W.*

Solomon. I can't find Miss Milly, mum.
Mrs. W. Is everybody disappearing? [*To Win.*] What is the meaning of this?
Win. The army, my dear, the army.
Col. What is the trouble?
Mrs. W. [R.] My servants have gone I don't know where, and I want them particularly.
Col. [L.] If you will permit it, the adjutant's man and mine will help you to hunt them up.
Sol. They're both gone off, Colonel.
Col. Gone off? Where?
Sol. Don't know, sir.
Col. Then let these stragglers be found. Tell the orderly at once.
Sol. Orderly's gone off, too, sir.
Col. [*Stage L., and back.*] By jove! A nice state of affairs, we'll soon put it to rights. Solomon! [*To Win. and Mrs. W.*] Will you permit me.
Win. Certainly, anything. [*Col. whispers to Sol., who runs out,* L. 2 E. *To Mrs. W.*] You wanted a house full of soldiers! How do you like it?
Mrs. W. It's not my fault, is it?

SYDAM *enters,* L. 2 E.

Col. Well, Sydam, have you found Dexter?
Sydam. I searched everywhere Colonel, but he seems to have disappeared. I'll try in this direction. [*Exits,* R. U. E.]
Col. The sooner the regiment leaves this place the better.
Win. Where can everybody be?
Col. We'll soon find out.

BUGLER *enters and stands,* L. 2 E., *at attention.*

Mrs. W. What are you going to do?
Col. You'll see directly. [*To Bugler.*] Sound the alarm.
[BUGLER *turns and sounds alarm, up stage, then marches off and sounds alarm, off stage, general alarm sounded in the distance.*]

PAUL *appears at window of summer-house.*

Paul. What's all this about? [*Sees the others and disappears.*]

MRS. BUNKER *and* TELKA *enter quickly.*

Mrs. Bunker and Telka. What is the matter? What has happened? [DOLF *crosses at back from* L. 2 E.]
Mrs. B. [*Intercepts him.*] Doctor, where is my daughter?
Dolf. Excuse me, I'm on duty.
Mrs. B. But you must know—

BUNKER *enters.*

Dolf. [*Coming down.*] I beg pardon. I've no time.

ROTH, *in military disguise, enters from* L., LINDA *with him; they start back on seeing so many persons.*

Linda. [*Frightened.*] Heavens! All these people.
Roth. [*Aside to her, up* L.] I'd had better get away at once. [*Tries to sneak off.*]
Col. [*Fiercely.*] Halt! [ROTH *pauses.*] Attention! Right about face! [ROTH *turns round and comes down.*]
Col. [*Same.*] Who are you, sir? [*Taking off Roth's hat.*]
Linda. [L., *up to Col.*] Please don't hurt him, it's only the apothecary.
Roth. Yes, I'm only the apothecary, and animated by a desire to—
Bunker. Only the— Pills and poison! [*Goes to him.*]
Mrs. B. The apothecary! With my daughter! Ah! [*Screams, goes after Bun.*] Oh, Linda! Linda!
·*Linda.* But pa—but ma! [ROTH *follows them.*]
Col. [*Crosses to* L.] Where is the lieutenant?
Paul. [*Springs out of window and salutes.*] Present, Colonel!
All. [*Surprised.*] The lieutenant!
Win. [*To Telka.*] This is my surprise, is it? [*Turns to*
5

Mrs. W., TEL. *hangs her head.*] That man was locked in there by your niece!

Mrs. W. By Telka! wretched girl! [*Screams and goes up,* TEL. *following her.*]

Tel. But aunt! Uncle!

MARY ANNE *and* SOPHIE *enter with soldiers.* COL. *calls attention, men salute and march up stage. Girls scream and run off.* SYDAM *enters with* MILLY, R. U. E.

Col. [*Stage,* R.] You, too, sir!

All. What, another?

Dolf. [*To Syd.*] What are you doing with that lady, sir?

Sydam. [*Advancing.*] All the same among the boys, you know.

Milly. Dear Dolf. [*They all go up quarreling,* SYD. *explaining to* COL. *General uproar. Bugle continues to play.*]

CURTAIN.

ACT V.

SCENE.—*Same as Act First.* WINTHROP *and* MRS. WINTHROP *discovered.*

Winthrop. [*Walking up and down.*] I told you just how it would be. ·

Mrs. Winthrop. [*Sitting at table,* L.] You make a great fuss about nothing.

Win. You call it nothing to have such a scandal occur in our house about your niece?

Mrs. W. But the girl admits everything.

Win. Of course she admits it, when I saw it with my own eyes. First she bars my way into the summer-hòuse, then tells a falsehood about a surprise in store for me, and then a lieutenant jumps out of the window! If that's the surprise for my birthday, I should like to see my Christmas present.

Mrs. W. It was the giddiness of a mere girl.

Win. She's getting a little too giddy. I'll take no more responsibility. You must write to her father at once to take her away.

Mrs. W. But, my dear—

Win. Not a word. I've given Milly warning, too. These New York damsels are much too advanced in their ideas for my New England views.

Mrs. W. Milly, what for?

Win. Oh, you didn't see that. She was discovered on the arm of one of the other lieutenants, who had a fight about her with the doctor.

Mrs. W. [*Jumps up.*] The doctor? That's impossible, the Bunkers told me that he was as good as engaged to Linda.

Win. Bah! These military gentlemen don't mind such little matters.

Mrs. W. [L.] I'm shocked!

Win. You will please to shock the cook and chambermaid, too, with their immediate discharge. I'll have a general clearing out this very day.

Mrs. W. My head's in a perfect whirl.

DOLF *enters,* L. D.

Dolf. [*Speaks back.*] All right. Good-bye. [*Turns.*] Good morning. [*To Win. and Mrs. W.*]

Mrs. W. [*Cool.*] Good morning.

Dolf. Last night's alarm so preoccupied us, that I have not had time to thank you for your kind reception.

Win. [*Cool.*] Don't mention it.

Mrs. W. I hope you enjoyed yourself, although for a young gentleman so fond of variety there were probably not young ladies enough.

Win. For a young gentleman who is said to be engaged, you are singularly impartial in your attentions.

Mrs. W. But perhaps you are one of those young gentlemen who do not take such matters seriously. Come, my dear. [*Takes Win.'s arm and looks at Dolf from top to toe.*] Good *morning*.

Win. [*Looking back over shoulder.*] Good morning! [*Exeunt,* R. D.]

Dolf. For a young gentleman who generally understands what people means, this is exceedingly puzzling.

SYDAM *enters,* C. L., *breathless.*

Sydam. [L.] Ah, there you are! What do you think? The answer's come.

Dolf. [R. C.] The answer?

Syd. [*Produces envelope.*] Yes, the telegram from Russia. From papa.

Dolf. What does he say?

Syd. I don't know. I havn't opened it yet.

Dolf. Why not, what are you waiting for?

Syd. Why, you see, the fact is, though I'm bold enough on ordinary occasions, I have a holy fear of this message. If the old man says yes—I'm in a nice mess.

Dolf. But you must learn the truth, sooner or later.

Syd. Certainly, and that's why I've come to you. I don't want to betray my emotions to parties not in the secret. Just stand ready to hold me, will you, in case I faint when I open it?

Dolf. Now then.

Syd. [*Crosses to* R., *opens dispatch, puts up glass, tries to read.*] What sort of language do you call this? Can you make it out?

Dolf. No. [*Looking at it.*]

Syd. Nor I!

Dolf. It is probably Russian.

Syd. Here's a nice business. How the deuce will we ever tell what's in it? What did they send it in Russian for?

Dolf. [L.] Why, you sent yours in English.

Syd. That's a different thing. English is a language that a fellow can understand. While this— Just listen to it. [*Crosses*

to L., *reads.*] " *Yeshuli*"—yes you lie—that's an unfortunate
beginning, isn't it? [*Reads.*] Yes you lie— " *Moya dotch
lubit barina tac on—*" Tack on! There's something encoura-
ging about that. I suppose it's equivalent to hold on! " *Tack
on morshat yaya imiyet.*" That don't sound so hopeful. There's
an uncertainty—a reserve—as if he was feeling his way. Perhaps the whole thing means: "Tack on till I come on!" eh?
Dolf. [*Taking dispatch.*] If it were only French or even
German.
Syd. Or Norwegian; I know lots of the boys who speak that
—as easy as Russian.
Dolf. There's nothing left but to show it to the young lady
herself.
Syd. Gad! That would never do.
Dolf. Then you'll have to burn it up and leave the country. .
Syd. I *have* done it this time, havn't I? I suppose I must
confide in her honor. She'll be angry, of course, but as I am
not going to marry her, it's only for once.
Dolf. I have an idea. There's Miss Milly. I've heard her
and Miss Telka once or twice exchange a few words in a language
that wouldn't be out of place in a Choctaw pow-wow, or an Irish
village.
Syd. [*Copies from dispatch into his book with pencil.*] It must
have been Russian, of course.
Dolf. Of course. They've been exchanging lessons. Suppose I show her the dispatch. I'll turn down your name and his,
and she'll be none the wiser after reading it.
Syd. [*Gives him dispatch.*] A capital idea. Find her at
once.
Dolf. [*Going.*] She's in the garden. [*Exits,* R. U. E.]
Syd. [*Following.*] Be sure you don't let her pump you.
[*Returns.*] It's an even chance that she gets at the secret in spite
of him.

PAUL *enters from* L. D.

Paul. Morning, Sydam!

SCIPIO *enters and stands at back.*

Syd. Morning! I say, you don't happen to understand Russian, do you?
Paul. [*Aside.*] What is he driving at! Are they going to
quiz? [*Eyes him furtively, crosses to* R.] No, he looks as innocent as a new laid egg. [*Aloud.*] No, I don't understand Russian; why do you ask?

Syd. Oh, nothing! Only the Doctor wanted to know. He's got something important. Day-day. [*Aside.*] I'll see if I can buy a Russian dictionary in the place. [*Exits*, c. l.]

Paul. Odd. [*To Scip.*] We march at two, Scipio; have everything packed.

Scipio. Bery nice quarters, dese, sah; pity we got to leave 'em. Do' I guess Newport's waitin' for us with open arms.

Paul. [*Going up with him.*] Now attend to my orders and keep your wits about you. [*Speaks to him, and* SCIP. *exits*, c. l.]

TELKA *enters*, R. D., *in riding habit, whip and gauntlets, terribly excited.*

Telka. No, I'll never, never stand this. [*Goes to table, rings angrily, and comes down, pulling up gauntlets.*] They shall know who I am. I'll take care of that. [*Crosses to* l.]

Paul. [*Comes down slowly.*] What is the matter, Miss Telka?

Tel. [*Up and down stage.*] If you knew how furious I am!

SOLOMON *enters*, c. l.

Solomon, put my ponies to the carriage. I'll drive to the station. [*Crosses to* R.]

Solomon. Yes, Miss. [*Aside.*] Everybody's catching it this morning. [*Exits*, c.]

Tel. [*To Paul.*] I am going home to my papa. I won't stay a moment longer in this house. To treat me—me in such a manner. [*Stamps her foot.*]

Paul. What has happened?

Tel. You should have heard the things uncle dared to say to me. [*Crosses to* l.] And yet I explained everything. I told him the whole truth. I never tell a falsehood, *never*, and yet he will not believe me. Oh! [*Cracks whip and stamps her foot.*]

Paul. Will you permit me to offer a little advice?

Tel. [*Not heeding.*] And there's no way to convince him. I'd just like to— [*Cracks whip.*] Durach!

Paul. [*Taking the whip, politely.*] Pardon me, the whip won't assist us in the least. [*Throws it on table.*] You are compromised by an unfortunate accident; there is only one way to mend matters, and if you will allow me to act in your behalf, everything will be arranged.

Tel. What can *you* do?

Paul. Ask your uncle formally for your hand.

Tel. Sir! [*Crosses to* R.]

Paul. Don't be alarmed; it is merely a strategical movement.

Tel. A strategical movement?

Paul. To exonerate you. *I* propose and you reject my offer; that will silence everybody. Am I not right?

Tel. [R.] Yes; but what will become of you?

Paul. Don't consider me in the least. I shall pocket my dismissal and depart happy in the thought of having rendered you a service. As a soldier, you know, I must get used to defeat among the other chances of war. I shall go and find your uncle. [*Crosses to* R.]

Tel. What! Now? Right away?

Paul. I have but one short hour left in your house, and must make the best use of it. [*Going, turns.*] Remember, I propose, and you say, "No." Don't forget—"No." [*Exits,* R.]

Tel. [*Solus.*] He proposes for me, and I am to say, "No." Oh, how miserable I am! [*Bursts into tears, crosses to* R.]

MILLY *enters, weeping, with letter,* R. U. E.

Milly. I have written to tell him everything—there is no other resource. [*Rings bell on table,* L.]

Tel. [*Aside, drying her tears.*] She shall not see me weep.

Mil. [*Controlling her emotion.*] Is that you, Telka? What is the matter? You've been crying.

Tel. I? Oh, no. Only my eyes smart.

Mil. So do mine. It must be something in the New England air. Are not my eyes red?

Tel. They look just as if you had been having a good cry.

Mil. [L.] I was sure of it.

Tel. And yet we are quite cheerful.

Mil. [*Sobs.*] I never felt happier.

Tel. [*Sobs, crosses to* L.] Isn't it funny?

Mil. [*Sobs.*] Very funny.

Tel. I—feel—so like laughing—

Mil. So—do—I— [*They suddenly burst into tears and fall into each others arms.*]

Tel. Oh, Milly! My heart is breaking.

Mil. I'm perfectly wretched. [*They cry, exchange handkerchiefs.*]

Wailing is heard, and SOPHIE *and* MARY ANNE *enter,* R. D., *crying aloud.*

Mary Anne. [*Sobbing.*] Did you ring, Miss?

Sophie. [*Sobbing.*] Oh, Miss Telka, can't you speak a kind word for me; I've been turned away.

Tel. [*Crying.*] Don't b—bother me.
Mary. Miss Milly, won't you speak for *me?*
Mil. [*Crying.*] Go away—I'm b—b—busy. [*All four cry.*]

ROTH *enters,* C. L., *in full dress, carries high white hat in his hand.*
He contemplates group.

Roth. [*Aside.*] I guess I've come at another bad time. [*Burst of grief from ladies.*] Everybody is in trouble. [*Looks at hat.*] So am I. That colored man mashed my hat. [*Another burst of grief.*] Don't cry, ladies, I can get it blocked for fifty cents. [*Aside.*] Mein Gott! it was a bad night. I hope you will pardon my intruding. [*To Sophie.*] Will you have the singular kindness to announce my visit to Mr. Winthrop?
Sophie. I dursn't do it, sir. I dursn't. [*Exits,* C. L.]
Mary. Nobody wouldn't go near him for their lives, sir. [*Exits,* C. L.]
Roth. [*To Mil.*] I am sorry, Miss, if you have to cry.
Mil. [*Weeping.*] So am I. [*Exits,* R. D.]
Roth. Miss Telka, I hope something dreadful has not come to somebody in the house.
Tel. [*Forcing calmness.*] Oh, no, nothing has happened. [*Exits,* R. U. E.]
Roth. That is comfortable. I wanted to speak to your uncle.

WINTHROP *enters,* R. D., *followed by* PAUL.

Roth. Ah! Mr. Winthrop, will you be so kind, I want a few moments of conversation. It is a matter most important. From my earliest childhood—
Winthrop. [*Kindly.*] I have an important matter on hand myself just at present, but if you will step into the next room, I'll be at your service presently.
Roth. Very good. [*Aside.*] Everything goes before me. I never get some one to listen to me till I take him by the collar. [*Exits,* L. D.]
Win. [*Calling off.*] Telka, come here.

TELKA *enters.*

My dear, Mr. Dexter has just made a surprising confession. He is a suitor for your hand.
Telka. [*Sadly,* L.] Indeed, sir!
Win. You know that the decision on this offer does not rest with me, but before communicating with your father, I felt bound to lay the proposal before you.

Tel. [*Same.*] You need not communicate with father, sir. [*To Paul.*] You will spare me painful explanations, Mr. Dexter. Much as your proposal honors me, I must answer at once with a decisive "No."

Win. [*Astonished,* c.] My dear Telka!

Paul. [*Crosses to* c.] Is this your final answer, Miss Telka?

Tel. [L.] Yes. [*Suppressing emotion.*] Do not be angry with me.

Paul. [*Steps back.*] I have no right to be angry.

Win. [*Crosses to Telka.*] You are a good girl, my dear, and I confess that I have done you a great injustice. [*Crosses to* L., *pats her cheek.*] I am heartily sorry, Mr. Dexter, but you heard the answer. [*Going, gives him his hand.*] I cannot help you. [*Exits,* L. D.]

Tel. [*Turns to give both hands to Paul.*] Thanks—thanks.

Paul. [*Kisses her hand.*] Farewell!

Tel. [*Calls after him.*] Mr. Dexter! You are leaving with the same bitter feelings you always cherished against me.

Paul. [*At door.*] You do not comprehend my feelings. It seems we shall never understand each other, [*Exits,* L. D.]

Tel. [*Makes a step, checks herself.*] Why on earth don't he make me understand, then. I'll give him any answer he wants. I'm sure he ought to see how ready I am to obey him in everything.

SYDAM *enters,* C. L.

Sydam. Excuse me—I was looking for the doctor.

Tel. [*Going,* R.] I have not seen him.

Syd. [*Aside.*] Now's my chance. I've got some of the words copied down. [*Looks at tablet.*] She won't suspect if I fire them off one by one instead of discharging by platoon. [*Aloud.*] Miss Telka, might I ask a great favor. Do you understand Russian?

Tel. Of course I do.

Syd. [L.] I *don't*, unfortunately, but I've taken a wonderful interest in the language. Would you kindly tell me the meaning of *dotch?*

Tel. Dotch?—that is Russian for daughter.

Syd. Daughter? Ah! One more please, what is *lubit?* [*He pronounces it loobit.*]

Tel. You mean *lubit* [l'youbit]—that is love.

Syd. [*Reflectively*] Love!

Tel. Any more?

Syd. No, thank you. I'm completely informed. Greatly obliged.

Tel. Don't mention it. [*Going, aside.*] I know somebody's daughter who is in love and very wretched. [*Exits,* R. D.]

Syd. [*Solus, sits* R. *of table.*] I'm just as wise as I was before. Love! Daughter! It seem's I've picked out the words of the least consequence. It's the little short ones that contain all the mischief. I wish I had inquired about "tack on!" [*Rises.*]

DOLF *enters,* C. R., *hurriedly, with slip of paper and the dispatch.*

Dolf. I've got it.
Syd. Got what?
Dolf. The translation.
Syd. [*Eagerly.*] Well?
Dolf. Prepare yourself. Papa sends you his blessing.
Syd. Gracious goodness! [*Falls in chair.*]
Dolf. Here you are. [*Reads.*] "If my daughter loves the gentleman, he may have her." Signed, Essoff. There. [*Gives dispatch and slip.*]
Syd. Well, it seems the old man is all right. [*Brightening.*] What a cheerful, straightforward, business-like father-in-law it is. [*Rises.*] It's a deuced shame. I've got everything but the bride. [*Crosses to* R.]
Dolf. [*Aside.*] Just my case. I've got everything but my wife.
Syd. I can't go back on this. Courage, old fellow. [*To Dolf.*] You stand by me and I'll give her the message. [*Goes into room,* R. D.]
Dolf. [*Looks around.*] I wish I had somebody to stand by me. I've got to confess everything or Milly will lose the only home she's got in the world. [*Goes cautiously to* L. *and looks into Win's. room.*] He's in there. Now for it. [*Exits,* L. D.]

Enter, C. L., MRS. WINTHROP, *with* MRS. BUNKER, BUNKER *and* LINDA *following.*

Mrs. Bunker. [*Comes down with Mrs. W.*] I don't know where else to go to for advice. You *must* help me to find out whether his attentions are really in earnest or not.
Mrs. Winthrop. Candidly, my dear friend, I believe not. Why, he's always in this house; he runs here every minute of the day. If he really took an interest in Linda he certainly wouldn't do that.
Mrs. B. I've noticed it. Can he be after Milly?

WINTHROP *enters from* L. *and goes directly to* BUN. DOLF *enters but stands near* L.

Mrs. W. [*To Mrs. B.*] I dare not tell you all that my husband saw last night. But it was perfectly scandalous.

Mrs. B. [*Glances at Dolf.*] And he looks so innocent.

Mrs. W. Appearances are the most deceitful things in the world.

Mrs. B. [*Looks at Linda.*] And Linda doesn't take the slightest notice of him.

Mrs. W. The girl has a proper spirit.

Bunker. [*Comes down to Mrs. B.*] My dear, Mr. Winthrop has an interesting communication to make.

Winthrop. [*Calmly*, L. C.] A certain young gentleman has begged my intercession in behalf of his proposal for your daughter.

Mrs. B. [*Glances at Dolf.*] He has spoken at last. I don't believe a thing they say against him.

Win. Have you any objection. [*Going to door*, L.]

Mrs. B. None whatever. I'm sure my daughter loves him.

Win. Then we won't keep him in suspense a moment longer. [*Exits*, L. D.]

Mrs. B. [*Rushes to Dolf.*] My dear child, why were you silent so long? I could have folded you to my heart. [DOLF *retreats up stage to avoid her—she follows him.*]

WINTHROP *enters*, L. D., *with* ROTH *by the hand, the latter, in his confusion, puts on his hat as he enters, not knowing what else to do with it.*

Winthrop. [*Pushes him to Bun.*] Embrace your father-in-law.

Roth. [*Rushes to Bun., who has his back towards him, and throws his arms over his shoulders. As* BUN. *turns,* ROTH *buries his head in his bosom, and so crushes his hat over his eyes.*] My second parent.

Dolf. [*At back, fighting off Mrs. B.*] My dear madam, this is a mistake.

Bun. [*To Roth, lifting up the latter's hat, which is crushed down over his ears.*] It's the druggist! What do you mean, sir, by calling me your second parent?

Win. [L.] Why not, if he's to be your son-in-law.

Bun. My son-in-law?

Mrs. B. [*Coming down* C., *bewildered.*] A mistake? What son-in-law?

Linda. [*Runs to Roth. To Mrs. B.*] We loved each other at first sight. We got the fever, the electric shock—everything at the same moment and both at once. [ROTH *embraces her.*] And all together.

Bun. You did! [*Looks at them, turns, crosses to* L. *To Mrs. B.*] Here's a pretty state of things! We'll have to make the best of this dose of physic.

Roth. And I have the honor to ask you, at first sight, that she will be my wife.

Mrs. B. [*To Bun.*] She'll be married, anyhow. [*Crosses to Roth.*] My dear child, let me fold you to my heart. [*Embraces him.*] Oh, why, why were you silent so long?

Roth. Why I was silent so long? Because, by gracious, I never get anyone to listen to me a minute when I tried to speak. [BUN. *and* MRS. B., ROTH *and* LINDA *go aside and converse.* LINDA *takes off Roth's hat and smoothes it carefully.*]

COLONEL *enters,* R. U. E., MILLY *on his arm. He gives her a letter as they converse.*

Colonel. I leave to you the pleasure of announcing his good fortune. We have secured his appointment.

Mil. [*Going to Dolf.*] Oh, my dear Dolf! [*Embrace.*]

Dolf. [*Alarmed.*] Sh! [*Motions her to be quiet.*]

Mrs. W. [R.] Miss Merritt! What is this?

Mil. [*Points to Dolf.*] This? This is the newly appointed surgeon of the New York Hospital—and this [*points to herself*] has the honor to be his wife. [*Curtseys.*]

Mrs. W. His wife!

Dolf. [*Kisses her.*] My good, patient, long-suffering and never-to-be-too-much loved wife! [*Both get* L.]

Win. [*To Mrs. W.*] I always thought she had a settled kind of way about her.

Mrs. W. Very remarkable for a young person whose prospects were so unsettled. Of course, we must congratulate them. Fah! How I hate deception! [*Goes to Mil., beaming.*] My dear child, your conduct and courage have won our life-long esteem. [*She and* WIN. *congratulate Dolf, then go back to* R.]

PAUL *enters,* L. D.

Col. Ah, Dexter! Are you ready to start?

Paul. [L.] At your service, Colonel. The regiment is drawn up in line, and the color guard are waiting your orders.

Col. Then we have only to say farewell! [*Goes to Win., and is surrounded by all on stage, except Paul and Tel.*]

TELKA *enters, R. D.*

Paul. [*Takes her hand.*] Will you permit me —
Telka. Must you go so soon?
Paul. Unfortunately. [*They look at each other, then look down. Their hands continue clasped while in this attitude.*]
Tel. [*Murmurs.*] Good-bye.
Paul. [*Same.*] Good-bye.
Tel. [*Looking up.*] You have been very good to me. I wish—at least, I can, return it in some measure by giving you a little advice, in my turn.
Paul. I should be most happy to have your advice.
Tel. Well, then, be more cautious in future.
Paul. How so?
Tel. Suppose I had taken you at your word and answered, "Yes."
Paul. Then I would have taken you at *your* word and been immeasurably happy.
Tel. [*Looks at him.*] Are you serious?
Paul. [*Ardently.*] Yes.
Win. [*Uneasy.*] What are they doing there?
Col. [*Not looking.*] Oh! saying farewell, I suppose. [*Secures Win.'s coat tail quietly to prevent his going to them.*]
Paul. Do you believe me? [*Seizes her hands.*]
Tel. [*Breathless.*] Yes. [*Puts her hands on his shoulder, and he clasps her to his heart.*]
Win. Telka, I'm surprised at you.
Tel. I'm surprised at myself, uncle!
Paul. [*To Win.*] I hope you won't be angry at hearing that we have changed our minds. Instead of retreating after my defeat, I return to the charge and win a signal victory. [*They go to group.*]

SYDAM *enters, R. D.*

Sydam. [*Aside.*] This is the moment to try my luck. [*Aloud.*] Miss Telka, will you have the goodness to read this telegram. It came this morning. [*Gives dispatch.*]
Tel. [*Joyfully, as she scans it.*] From my father! [*Reads.*] "If my daughter loves the gentleman, he shall have her."
Syd. Quite correct.
Tel. But who telegraphed to papa?
Syd. I did.
Tel. [*Effusively.*] For your comrade! [*Grasps his hand.*] You are, indeed, a friend! [*Turns away, leaving Syd. astounded.*]

Col. [*Comes down to Win.*] I know Dexter. He will make an excellent husband.

Syd. [*Aside, crosses to* L.] Dexter! I'm overboard again.

Win. Nothing can be settled without her father's consent.

Tel. [*Gives dispatch.*] Mr. Sydam has telegraphed for it in the kindest manner. [*Translates dispatch for Win.*]

Paul. [*Rushes to Syd.*] My dear fellow. [*All stare at Syd.*]

Syd. [*Composed.*] Yes, good idea, wasn't it?

Tel. He foresaw everything!

Win. It's wonderful!

Col. Astonishing instance of penetration.

Syd. Ahem! [DOLF, *who has come down to him, gives him slight kick.*]

Dolf. [*Aside to him.*] Ahem! [SYD. *returns the kick; they separate.*]

Paul. [*Clasping Syd.'s hand.*] And *I* thought you were my rival.

Syd. Yes. It don't matter which has the lady—all the same among the boys, you know! [COL., C., *all others in attitudes of farewell; roll of drum heard.*]

Col. [C.] Now, gentlemen! Time to be off. [*Takes leave of Win. and Mrs. W.*] Let me hope that the Passing Regiment leaves a good name behind it.

Mrs. W. Better than that, Colonel. It takes a good character with it. [*Distant march heard, very piano.*]

Paul. [*To Tel.*] It won't be for long. Two days at Newport, another to return. Another to tell my mother the good news—and bring her with me to see her daughter.

Tel. Is she very good and very kind? What will she say?

Paul. Much the same as the good soul who sent this cable message. If my son loves the lady, I will love her.

Mil. [L., *to Dolf.*] It seems like a dream. I feel as if I were walking in my sleep.

Dolf. Don't wake up. Go on and dream of our new home. I've had my eye on a little house for ever so long. Be in town Tuesday, and we'll walk in our sleep to the landlord and get a lease for a dream of ten years with renewals.

Linda. [*To Roth.*] Oh, we can't be married for months yet.

Roth. We must. I explain to your parents it is better for business. I am not right in my mind till I have got you. If I go on this way for months, I mix things and kill some people.

Linda. Well, not under four weeks at the very least.

Roth. Two weeks. I fill the wrong bottles if it's more than two weeks.

Col. Gentlemen! Good-bye.

Syd., Paul, Dolf. Good-bye.
Milly, Win. and Mrs. W. Good-bye.
Tel. One little word more. [*To the audience.*]

> Dear friends, whose girlhood, as I plainly see,
> Allies you in sweet sisterhood with me,
> Heartache, like headache, is a common ill;
> Don't hide it, for you may not if you will.
> The rosy god has darts that nicely speed,
> When once they hit, why own at once you bleed;
> And take this lesson from our play to-night,
> Tho' love is blind, acknowledge him at sight.

CURTAIN.

THE

PASSING REGIMENT

A COMEDY OF THE DAY, IN FIVE ACTS.

(From the German of G. von Moser and Franz von Schonthau.)

BY

AUGUSTIN DALY.

AS ACTED AT DALY'S THEATRE FOR THE FIRST TIME,
NOVEMBER 10TH, 1880.

NEW YORK:
PRINTED AS MANUSCRIPT ONLY, FOR THE AUTHOR.
1884.

.